THE PASSING OF MR QUINN

'THE DETECTIVE STORY CLUB is a clearing house for the best detective and mystery stories chosen for you by a select committee of experts. Only the most ingenious crime stories will be published under the THE DETECTIVE STORY CLUB imprint. A special distinguishing stamp appears on the wrapper and title page of every THE DETECTIVE STORY CLUB book—the Man with the Gun. Always look for the Man with the Gun when buying a Crime book.'

Wm. Collins Sons & Co. Ltd., 1929

Now the Man with the Gun is back in this series of COLLINS CRIME CLUB reprints, and with him the chance to experience the classic books that influenced the Golden Age of crime fiction.

THE DETECTIVE STORY CLUB

FURTHER TITLES IN PREPARATION

THE PASSING OF MR QUINN

THE BOOK OF THE FILM

ADAPTED FROM A SHORT STORY
BY

AGATHA CHRISTIE

NOVELISED BY

G. ROY McRAE

WITH AN INTRODUCTION BY
MARK ALDRIDGE

COLLINS
CRIME
CLUB

COLLINS CRIME CLUB
An imprint of HarperCollins*Publishers*
1 London Bridge Street
London SE1 9GF
www.harpercollins.co.uk

This edition 2017

First published in Great Britain in The Novel Library by
The London Book Co., an imprint of Wm Collins Sons & Co. Ltd 1928

Novelisation © HarperCollins*Publishers* Ltd 1928
Introduction © Mark Aldridge 2017

The publishers would like to thank Agatha Christie Ltd
for their co-operation in the publication of this edition.

A catalogue record for this book is available from the British Library

ISBN 978-0-00-824396-8

Typeset in Bulmer MT Std by
Palimpsest Book Production Ltd, Falkirk, Stirlingshire
Printed and bound by CPI Group (UK) Ltd, Croydon, CR0 4YY

INTRODUCTION

OF the many publications that have been associated with (but not written by) Agatha Christie, *The Passing of Mr Quinn* is certainly one of the most curious—and, until now, one of the rarest. Originally published in 1928, the book is actually a novelisation of the silent film of the same title, which had been released the same year and was the very first screen adaptation of an Agatha Christie story. The film itself is now lost, along with its script, meaning that this tie-in publication is our best insight into this filmmaking first. The movie was publicised as an adaptation of Christie's short story 'The Passing of Mr Quinn', which had introduced the charming but mysterious stranger Harley Quinn, a man whose sudden appearance motivates characters to untangle a mystery that has been hanging over them for many years.

The timeline for the story might initially seem to be reasonably straightforward: Agatha Christie's original short mystery 'The Passing of Mr Quinn' was published in the March 1924 edition of *The Grand Magazine* before being adapted into the July 1928 film that used the same title. The film's new interpretation of the mystery was then novelised as this book, *The Passing of Mr Quinn*, and Christie's original short story was later published in April 1930 as the opening part of the short story collection *The Mysterious Mr Quin*, where it was renamed 'The Coming of Mr Quin', perhaps to differentiate it from the film and this novelisation. However, the development of this story is a little more complicated than this timeline may indicate.

One point is immediately obvious to those familiar with the original short story—the film and its novelisation diverge significantly from Christie's narrative. In her original story, a mysterious death in the past is raised in a discussion amongst friends, who are spurred on by Quinn to make sense of the events. The film takes the same death as its starting point of the dramatisation, but after the main suspect is cleared it moves off in a wildly different direction as it emphasises the romantic relationship between two key characters and the appearance of a mysterious stranger.

In order to make sense of *The Passing of Mr Quinn*'s journey between media we need to begin by looking at its original magazine appearance in 1924. The first thing to note about this version is the title, which spells the titular character with two 'n's. This is consistent with the later film, but not with Christie's book of the short stories, which established 'Quin' as the definitive spelling. The title of both the film (which is often misspelled in articles) and this novelisation is not an aberration, then, but a reproduction of the original character's name as it had appeared in the first four stories in *The Grand Magazine*. In fact, it was only when *The Story-teller* magazine published the next six stories that the spelling changed from Mr Quinn. Debuting in the Christmas 1926 issue and appearing monthly under the general headline 'The Magic of Mr Quin', this 'New series of brilliant mystery stories' established Quin as Christie's third serial character after Hercule Poirot and Tommy & Tuppence. (Miss Marple did not appear anywhere until December 1927.)

The title is not the only change that occurred between the original publication of the story and its later appearance in the book collection of Quin stories some six years later. *The Grand Magazine*'s original 'The Passing of Mr Quinn' is several hundred words shorter than the version that would eventually be published in the book as 'The Coming of Mr Quin', and it is clear that Christie substantially redrafted the mystery before handing it over to Collins for *The Mysterious Mr Quin* collection. Some sections, such as the beginning, are almost completely rewritten, while elsewhere smaller details change. For example, Christie aficionados may notice that Alex Portal from 'The

Coming of Mr Quin' is named Alec in this 1928 novelisation, but this is in fact the original name of the character as printed in 1924. Elsewhere, Mr Satterthwaite ages from 57 in the original magazine to 62 in the collected short stories, while in terms of tone there is marginally more emphasis on Quinn's qualities as a quiet manipulator in the original text.

A unique feature of *The Grand Magazine* story was the addition of line drawings to illustrate key moments, including the first visual representation of Mr Quinn. However, it strictly adheres to the text's description of him being in 'motoring clothes', and as a consequence his attire of a sensible rain jacket and flat cap does make him seem rather less mysterious than the reader may otherwise have imagined.

It was therefore this original version of the debut Quinn story that was adapted by director and screenwriter Leslie Hiscott to form the basis of the film *The Passing of Mr Quinn*. The picture was made quickly and inexpensively at Twickenham Studios by Julius Hagen Productions for film distributor Argosy in order to satisfy new demands that a certain percentage of domestic film productions should, amongst other things, be based on a scenario by British writers. *The Passing of Mr Quinn* would be one of the first of many 'quota quickies', made specifically to satisfy the new regulations rather than as the result of any particular artistic or business desire for the title. In the event, the film of *The Passing of Mr Quinn* took only a few elements of the original short story to form the basis of its bizarre and somewhat illogical—but nevertheless entertaining—screenplay that would not only veer away from the original narrative but also completely reinvent the title character. To say more would ruin the surprise of the events as they unfold in the following book, but suffice to say there is little in common between the Mr Quinn of this story and Agatha Christie's original character.

The film was given a relatively limited release, and was not well received. On the whole, critics found it overlong (at 100 minutes) and somewhat preposterous, with particular disdain

The Passing of Mr. Quinn

should never have been allowed to do such a thing in my young days."

"*Autre temps, autre mœurs,*" said Conway, smiling.

He was a tall, soldierly-looking man. Both he and Evesham were much of the same type—honest, upright, kindly men with no great pretensions to brains.

"In my young days we all joined hands in a circle and sang ' Auld Lang Syne,'" continued Lady Laura. "' Should Auld Acquaintance be Forgot '—so touching, I always think the words are."

Evesham moved uneasily.

"Oh! drop it, Laura," he muttered. "Not *here!*"

He strode across the wide hall where they were sitting and switched on an extra light.

"Very stupid of me," said Lady Laura, *sotto voce.* "Reminds him of poor Mr. Capel, of course. My dear, is the fire too hot for you?"

Eleanor Portal had made a brusque movement.

"Thank you. I'll move my chair back a little."

What a lovely voice she had—one of those low, murmuring, echoing voices that stay in your memory, thought Mr. Satterthwaite. Her face was in shadow now. What a pity!

From her place in the shadow she spoke again.

"Mr.—Capel?"

"Yes. The man who originally owned this house. He shot himself, you know—oh! very well, Tom dear, I won't speak of it unless you like. It was a great shock for Tom, of course, because he was here when it

Framed in the doorway stood a man's figure, tall and slender. "I must apologise for this intrusion," said the stranger, in a pleasant, level voice.

for the portrayal of Quinn himself by Vivian Baron. Nevertheless, some commentators found elements of the mystery intriguing and commended it for the interesting visual presentations of some scenes. However, the harshest critic was possibly Agatha Christie herself. The specific details of the agreement that allowed an adaption—and then a novelisation—of her story are lost to us, as no paperwork survives, but we can infer a great deal from the circumstantial evidence. For one thing, although this book's title is the same as both the original short story and the film, the text renames Quinn once more, this time to 'Quinny', with a curious disclaimer at the beginning of the text requesting that readers understand that this is the same character as seen in the film. (It appears to have been a last-minute alteration, in that one instance of Quinn rather than Quinny survived unchanged in the text.)

We can assume that this further change of name was made in order to assuage Christie's displeasure at the appearance of the book—from her own publishers, no less—although it did not prevent her name from being featured prominently on the dustjacket. Christie seems to have been unaware that she had signed away the rights to novelise the film. This annoyed her greatly and informed her later business dealings. When her agent, Edmund Cork, formulated a (later abandoned) deal with MGM in the 1930s to film some of her works, she was insistent that the contract should make it clear that, while the studio may make original mysteries for the screen featuring her characters, they were not to be novelised.

Nevertheless, such discomfort came too late for *The Passing of Mr Quinn*, and the novelisation was printed—although only once—as part of The Novel Library, an inexpensive collection of small-format books consisting mainly of reprints of well-known titles by the likes of H.G. Wells, Jack London and A.E.W. Mason, plus lesser-known books that had been turned into films. In the event, Christie's displeasure seemed hardly worth the effort as both book and film of *The Passing of Mr*

Quinn sank without a trace, although the picture was seen as far away as Australia.

The novelisation itself often feels like an Agatha Christie mystery as reimagined by someone with no real affinity for the intricacies of the genre. Instead, it firmly leads with melodrama above all else. As for the person who performed this reworking, there is little to say, as the credited author of the book, G. Roy McRae, has no other publications to their name and is almost certainly a pseudonym for a freelancer or staff writer—although we cannot dismiss the possibility that it was Leslie Hiscott, the film's director and adapter, changing his name to avoid bearing the brunt of Christie's ire.

Whoever the author was, they were less interested in nuance and character than Christie was, but showed a keen emphasis on the more salacious elements of murder, relationships and the impact of crime. Indeed, some elements (including Quinn himself) are suitably macabre for the increasingly horror-tinged popular movies of the time; one could imagine Lon Chaney playing the part as described. However, as a mystery, there are some clumsily executed changes of scenario and loose ends that Christie herself would never have allowed, while the introduction of such elements as an untraceable poison break the code of conventions adhered to by the major mystery writers of the era. *The Passing of Mr Quinn* provides the reader with an unpredictable journey through various scenarios and locations, changing genre along the way, until we reach the final act of the story having little understanding of what mystery we are trying to solve, although it's hard not to be swept up in the drama of piecing together the story that links some unusual characters. In the end, according to contemporary accounts, the story's resolution works rather better on the page than it did on the screen, and while *The Passing of Mr Quinn* is a curiosity, it is certainly an interesting one.

MARK ALDRIDGE
March 2017

THE PASSING OF MR QUINN

THE BOOK OF THE FILM BY G. ROY McRAE

THIS dramatic film thriller is adapted from a novel by Agatha Christie, the world's greatest woman writer of detective stories. It provides a new and original type of thriller since three persons in the story could be reasonably suspected of a motive which would prompt them to poison the most hateful villain who ever crossed the pages of fiction. Who, then, poisoned the cruel and sinister Professor Appleby? Derek Capel, his neighbour, in love with the Professor's wife, Eleanor? Vera, the house-parlour-maid, Appleby's mistress? Or was it Eleanor Appleby herself? This is a story full of dramatic moments and thrilling suspense. It will keep you guessing until the final page.

NOTE

READERS are requested to note that Mr Quinny of this book is the same person as the Mr Quinn of the film.

CHAPTER I

Professor Appleby listened.

He stood in the centre of his study, his hands in the pockets of his dinner jacket, and a curious half smile on his lips as he listened intently.

He heard nothing, for his house was silent as the grave.

If there had been any sound Professor Appleby would assuredly have heard it, for amongst the rows of valuable books that lined the walls of his study there were dummy books. Dummies that held microphones which could carry any sound made in any room of that house to its master in the centre study.

Professor Appleby alone had knowledge of this. His wife, Eleanor, was terrified of his omniscience of everything that went on in the house. She knew that she could not give an order to the servants without the professor knowing of it. It was one of Professor Appleby's subtle means of cruelty, and it had contributed a great deal towards the state of nervous exhaustion to which she had become prostrated.

After listening for a moment or two Professor Appleby laughed softly. It was a precise, mirthless sound like the tinkle of ice in a glass.

Satisfied that, as yet, all was quiet in his house, he crossed the thick pile red carpet to the broad mahogany desk in the centre of his study. It was a study indicative of his tastes, for it was furnished with every luxury and refinement, yet it bristled with the bizzarre. The bookcases contained exquisite vellum-bound volumes, old editions, and strange works of foreign publishers. A glass-door cupboard on one side of the room held chemicals and test-tubes, giving the study the appearance of a laboratory, which was offset by the cushions which lay on

1

chairs and settee, the soft-shaded lamp and the glowing radiator which gave the big room generous warmth.

On the carpet near the mahogany desk was a stout wicker-work basket. Professor Appleby, with a strange smile twitching his lips, bent over it, and untying a string lifted a lid. He straightened himself with a huge Haje snake coiling and wriggling in his arms and round his shoulders, and he laughed again softly.

It was a startling and repellant sight in that room of luxury and taste. The red curtains were drawn over the window to shut out the gathering dusk, and all was silent in the study save for the ticking of the clock and Professor Appleby's long-repressed breath. It was a ticklish job he was doing.

After a few moments of manipulation with instruments from a case on the desk, Professor Appleby jerked erect, satisfied that his experiment was coming to a successful issue. The smile on his lips was scarcely pleasant.

Spite of his huge, elephantine figure there was a suggestion of pantherish power in Professor Appleby's movements. Now once again he seized the snake with cruel, strong white fingers just below its head, and bent over it with an instrument in his other hand.

He had a gross white face that appeared to be carefully attended, and very finely pencilled eyebrows that had a satanic uplift; an extremely strong nose and jaw, and lips that were a red, twitching line. A monocle gleamed in his right eye, and those eyes were as bright as a snake's themselves, holding the heavy-lidded droop of mastery.

Such was Professor Appleby, a monstrous figure of ebony and white in his dinner suit, as he wrestled under the soft-shaded lamp with the Haje spitting snake.

There sounded all at once a slight hiss. The Haje's long body wriggled and coiled sinuously, so that its black and white diamond markings seemed to blur. A glass vessel fell to the carpet, knocked over by the snake in its struggles, and Professor Appleby's monocle dropped on its black cord as he smiled grimly.

He had forgotten for a moment that Doctor Portal had arranged to call that evening on Eleanor, his wife—forgotten it in the fascination of the strange experiment he had been conducting.

The Haje, a fierce species of African cobra, had just exercised its remarkable and disconcerting habit of ejecting poison from its mouth to a considerable distance, and the professor had collected the discharge and had drawn the cobra's fangs. It was now completely harmless, its poison-spitting propensities stopped for all time.

The professor dropped into a chair, watching the snake's convulsions a moment, while he wiped his white hands fastidiously with a handkerchief.

There were tiny beads of perspiration on his forehead. For all his coolness he had known the experiment to be a dangerous one.

It was such experiments as this that had gained for Professor Appleby a reputation entirely enviable in the world of science and research. He was a noted expert in poisons and a pathologist of world-wide repute. Such ability—in the eyes of the world, at least—condoned a personal reputation that was somewhat dubious.

If the consensus of opinion was that Professor Appleby was the most brilliant scientist of his day, it was also freely rumoured that he had paid the penalty of genius. The dividing line between genius and insanity is a very thin one, and Professor Appleby was very much on the borderline: he had a cruel and sinister side to his character which could scarcely be called normal.

There were rumours current of strange habits he had acquired during his long sojourn in the East. Gossip has many votaries in an English country village, and Professor Appleby's house, the Lodge, discreetly retired though it was, behind a long avenue of trees, was the object of much curiosity and an astonishing penetrative insight on the part of the villagers.

'How he ever married her. I don't know'—this referred to the gracious woman with hair of golden-brown and large, pathetic brown eyes who was occasionally to be seen flitting through the village with flushed face averted as though she knew she were an object of pity. Local opinion was unanimous about Eleanor Appleby. Two years before she had been a girl of breathless beauty; now it was evident that she walked with fear. She had been induced by the persuasions of her mother and her friends to accept the brilliant Professor Appleby as suitor—and now she was paying the cost of her husband's erratic genius.

There was a great deal more gossip. Stories of his cruelty, and of his preference for the society of other women. How these got about in the village it is difficult to tell, for Professor Appleby was careful to throw a barricade of secrecy around the Lodge. His menage consisted of two domestics, a white-haired cook whose frightened manner and consistent head-shaking was the answer to any curious question about life at the Lodge, an old gardener and handy man who for some reason of his own had the silence of the sphinx in his tongue, and Vera, the house parlourmaid. Vera? Well, Vera, too, may have had her own reasons for not talking.

Yet rumour had got about, and Professor Appleby was conscious of it. He was sensitive about it, too, sensitive as a man who has some secret vice. As he stood back from the snake which was now twisting to the carpet, a sudden savagery flitted across his gross, white face. It was quickly eradicated. Indeed, he crossed the carpet, softly as a cat, and looked at his own reflection in a mirror, screwed his monocle in his eye and wagged a white forefinger warningly at himself.

No one must see it. No one must guess.

He turned away from the mirror again, and tried to capture elusive memories of an astonishing outburst he had made at a medical board in London a week before. What had he done—what had he said? Really he ought not to do these things. He must keep a closer guard over himself.

He thrust his hands deep in the pockets of his trousers and

stood with feet apart, his chin sunk as he stared with glittering eyes at the cobra.

Suddenly he started.

Through the microphone concealed in one of the dummy books had come distinctly the sound of a knock at the front door of the Lodge, then faintly the sounds of the maid's footsteps and the opening of the door. Then voices; a man's deep and hearty, and a woman's confused low tones.

Professor Appleby's brows drew together, and somehow the faint contortion gave the heavy white face with its bright eyes a terribly sinister expression. The professor had that type of gross face that many exceedingly clever men possess; to watch its fleeting expressions provided a fascinating, if rather frightening study.

He listened. It was evident that those in the hall were taking care not to be overheard, for their voices sounded in undertone to their footsteps moving towards the drawing-room. The microphone made of their conversation a mere confused buzz, and only now and then did a word sound with clarity.

Professor Appleby knew that his wife and Doctor Alec Portal were talking together in the drawing-room.

He caught snatches through the microphone, chiefly in the man's voice.

'. . . You must not . . . then leave him . . . For your own sake I beg of you, Eleanor.'

The listening professor smiled beneath frowning brows. Quickly he picked up the writhing, harmless cobra and stowed it away in the wickerwork basket, then once more wiping his hands in his handkerchief, he crossed the carpet, lithe and buoyant to an astonishing degree in a man of such heavy build.

Softly traversing the passage between the study and the drawing-room, he opened the door suddenly, and the two inside the room, seated on a settee near the window, looked up startled to see him regarding them from the threshold.

In the woman his presence caused instant and dire confusion. Eleanor Appleby snatched away the delicately moulded hand that Doctor Portal had been holding whilst in pursuance of his professional duties he felt her pulse, and that same hand went like a fluttering bird to her heart. She paled—it was pitiable that swift pallor that drained her face of every vestige of colour— and her dilated eyes stared at her husband whilst she trembled.

Doctor Alec Portal looked swiftly from Professor Appleby to the beautiful, stricken creature on the settee beside him, and a frown knit his brows as he sprang to his feet.

Across the empty space of the room the two men measured glances. Doctor Alec Portal's level-gray eyes did not waver, though in those few seconds he knew that rumour was right about Professor Appleby.

His eyes were restless, unnaturally bright under the frowning brows; his mouth twitched ever so slightly. He held himself well in check, of course, but the cruel glow that showed in his eyes as he looked at Eleanor could not belong to a quite normal man.

It was Doctor Alec Portal who spoke first.

'Professor Appleby, I believe?' he said in icy tones.

These two had crossed each other's path many times, yet had never spoken. In public Professor Appleby was an extremely dignified and even ponderous man, and scarcely likely to take notice of a country medico.

Alec Portal, however, looked far different from the traditional village doctor. He had bought the country practice at Farncombe merely as a diversion from his wealth and because medicine appealed to him. Earlier in life he had selected the army as a career, and he bore the stamp of it unquestionably.

Hardly yet in his forties, he stood some six feet in his socks, with a fair, tanned and clean-cut face that could be unbelievably boyish and handsome, and at times implacably stern.

Stern he appeared now as Professor Appleby crossed the room towards him. It was quite obvious from the professor's attitude, the sneering smile upon his lips, that he was going to commit one of those breaches of good taste for which he was becoming notorious.

'Every one in Farncombe knows that I am Professor Appleby, I think,' he said with icy contempt. 'And also that my wife is—well, mine.'

Doctor Alec Portal flushed.

He could not mistake the implied allusion. It was, in fact, coldly brutal, and he heard a little gasp from the settee. Professor Appleby was regarding him with a provocative and sneering smile, and Doctor Portal controlled his rising anger with difficulty.

'That is exactly my point,' he said harshly. 'I am Doctor Alec Portal, as you know, and I am in attendance upon Mrs Appleby in a medical capacity. I am glad to have the opportunity of seeing you tonight, professor, for I wish to warn you that your wife is far from well.'

Professor Appleby's eyebrows shot up.

'Indeed,' he said suavely, 'that is news to me. I have qualifications as a medical man myself, and I should have said that Mrs Appleby is enjoying the best of health. Still—' he crossed the carpet, and took his wife's hand, feeling her pulse with a judicial air.

His back was half-turned to Alec Portal, but, indeed, the young doctor was not exercising any special vigilance for the moment, and therefore he did not observe the cruel pressure of Professor Appleby's strong fingers upon his wife's arm.

Alec Portal was caught up in a sudden strange wonder. As the professor had crossed the room Eleanor Appleby had cast a swift glance of appeal to him. And for a breathless moment a galvanic force that Doctor Portal had never before experienced and did not understand, swept through him.

He knew that he was trembling a little. He believed it was through the tensity of the situation, for he was sure that a demon raged in the breast of this man whose intellectual achievements had amazed the scientific world. A demon of merciless cruelty, urging him, driving him to outrageous acts of subtle torture.

And yet—what was this wild thrill that raged through him

as he stared at Eleanor Appleby? It was as if he had suddenly awakened to something new and wonderful.

Her eyes were cast down, and she was trembling violently, and her childish face was pitiful. Yet, perhaps because of her extreme pallor, she looked as fresh and sweet as a dew-drenched rose at dawn. Alec Portal continued to stare at her. That brute's wife, he told himself! And with the soft lamplight pouring on her flawless face and brown-gold hair she looked a very dainty and pretty little wife.

So pretty, indeed, as her lashes trembled against her smooth, pale cheeks that a voice whispered madly within him of things he had never dreamed.

All at once a little gasp broke from her. She looked up at the man who held her wrists so cruelly; her eyes lit with anguish.

'Oh, please—please stop!' she whispered.

Doctor Alec Portal heard it. He started forward, his handsome face working convulsively. But at the same moment Professor Appleby released his wife, and turned. There was sardonic amusement, and something else unfathomable, lurking in the gleaming eyes that mockingly challenged the doctor's.

'I must thank you for your solicitude,' he drawled, 'but I find my wife quite well. In any case, I think I should prefer myself to choose her medical attendant if she were ill—one, say, who is not quite so impetuous, and who understands better the etiquette of his profession.'

Aflame with anger, Doctor Portal was on the point of making some hasty retort, but checked himself in time. There was something besides his own personal feelings to be considered. This girl—for she was little more—was being driven to breaking point.

His eyes, narrowed to shining slits, blazed at the cold, sneering face.

'I warn you, sir, that you may have a very serious matter to answer for,' he said between clenched teeth. 'Mrs Appleby needs rest and change. She is near to nervous prostration, and must take a holiday. It is the worst case of nerves I have ever encountered.'

Professor Appleby drew himself up. His smooth, white face lost its sneering smile and became terrible.

For a moment he glared at the young doctor, and his eyes held the burden of his storming and reviling soul.

'Nerves, eh?' he grated, like a bug spitting venom, 'Doctor, from my own observations, I should say it was a case of the heart.'

He walked to the door and flung it open. For all that he was holding it under control, his rage was staggering.

'Get out,' he said thickly. 'D'you hear? Get out! Or, by the Lord Harry, there'll be a case of horsewhipping for the villagers to gossip again. And please have the decency to leave my wife alone in future. And don't come near my house again—understand.'

Alec Portal stared at him hard.

Not since his schoolboy days had he felt such an overwhelming, primitive impulse to punish another human being. He would dearly have liked to have wiped the disdain from that gross face with a thudding left. But in the end he shrugged and gathered up his ulster and cap. He was in an impossible position, and the only thing he could do was to leave with dignity.

Bestowing a formal little bow upon Eleanor, who sat with eyes cast down, shamed, he strode past the malevolent figure of Professor Appleby at the door and went from the house.

But as he opened the front door, he heard the sound of a stifled sob, and he looked back, startled, questioning. She was in there with that brute, crying. Should he go back? Should he kill the husband?

His heart was filled with a cold, murderous rage. He took a grip of himself, and was astonished. What was the matter with him? Was he himself tonight?

He closed the door, and strode away into the gathering dusk, pulling his coat collar up and his broad-visored cap down. He was almost afraid of himself, afraid of his own thoughts and desires. Something primitive and lawless had woke to life in Doctor Alec Portal, who had always thought himself so cold.

He walked quickly, trying to shake off his thoughts. One thing was obvious. He must never go near the house that contained Professor Appleby's wife again. Passion and love had been awakened in his deep strong nature at last. And it was love for another man's wife!

Even now he fought against a wild impulse to turn back. All his chivalry urged him to protect her from that brute. But with a resolute gritting of his teeth he strode on.

His eyes were bleak as they penetrated the gathering dusk.

'Heavens,' he muttered; 'it's a funny old world!'

Doctor Alec Portal had scarce closed the front door behind him when Professor Appleby returned to the drawing-room. Outwardly he was calm and collected. His gleaming monocle was screwed in his right eye, and he tried to restrain the twitching of his lips.

Eleanor, his wife, was still sitting on the settee, racked by a tempest of half-stifled sobs.

He watched her from the doorway with a sneering smile.

Her beauty no longer moved him. Indeed, beauty in all living things impelled in him an awful, mad lust to destroy. That was the kink in this brilliant scientist's brain. He had been known to sit for hours plucking the petals from one choice bloom after another. As a boy, one of his absorbing hobbies had been the collection of butterflies and birds' eggs, and he had plundered nests ruthlessly and taken a peculiar delight in the destruction of Nature's most beautiful creatures.

Thus it was with his wooing of Eleanor.

From the first, her beauty and peculiar charm had exercised a fatal fascination for him. He desired her as he had wanted the butterfly when a boy—to pin down and destroy. He had never been the lover. And on the very day of their marriage had come frightful disillusion for Eleanor Appleby.

She had married not a man, but a fiend who was capable of exercising the most cunning and subtle forms of cruelty.

Whether it was from knowledge of the law's remorselessness,

or his own desire to play with his victim, Professor Appleby had adopted a gradual process of destruction. His constant spying on her, his taunts, his subtle and hideous little cruelties, all were tearing at Eleanor Appleby's nerves. Visibly she had lost her fragrant charm, and was listless, apathetic, like a drooping flower. But even she had not known how near she was to nervous exhaustion until recently, and then in a panic she had sent for Doctor Alec Portal.

Professor Appleby threw back his head in a mirthless, almost silent laugh.

He felt queerly elated—pleased. Something seemed to snap in his brain, and the result of it was that he felt as a man does who has tossed off a bumper of champagne to which he is unaccustomed. When he let himself go there were compensations to this queer kink in his brain. He knew he was not normal, but it was a very pleasant state.

He commenced to lash her with his tongue.

'So this is what you do!' he said in that thin, precise tone with which he addressed a medical board. 'You, whom I thought were a faithful wife—you to whom I have given the best in me. To think that you are a light-o'-love, Eleanor . . .'

He had chosen the words with devilish cunning. She started as though fire had touched her, and looked up.

'Oh, yes,' he said with his thin, mirthless smile. 'I heard it, even in my room. He was urging you to go away—to leave me—'

With a faint moan she put up her hand as if to stay the cruel words. But he stepped forward and dashed it aside, glowering down at her.

'Say something,' he commanded with brutal violence. 'What is that man to you?'

She was trembling violently.

'I—I—you don't understand—'

She got no further. His white hands went out, gripping her neck and shoulder. Against all her resistance she was swung gently, powerfully this way and that. There was a softness in that great strength, but she knew it could shake the life out of her, crush her with but little effort.

'Listen,' he said evenly and grimly. 'The rest of the world lies outside this house. The house is mine, and so is everything in it,' he added. For a fraction of a moment he stared at her, and in his glittering eyes she read what his words but thinly disguised.

She was shuddering violently at that look of sheer, animal gloating—it made her sick with terror.

He had changed now. And the metamorphosis in him was more frightening than any she had ever known. For he became the ardent wooer.

She almost cried out when he stretched out his arms. Then he caught her to him, and she was crushed against him in a savage embrace that nearly suffocated her. Again and again she tried to cry out, to push him away from her. But his lips were seeking hers.

His arms were around her, and the touch of her soft, girlish form suddenly seemed to set him afire with the desire for possession.

'You witch!' he said hoarsely. 'You can't get away from me now. You're mine—mine, d'you hear?'

Sick with terror she nearly fainted. A low cry broke from her lips.

'Oh, please . . . please . . . have mercy . . . If you have any chivalry in you have pity on me.'

But he only laughed at her.

'Little wife; there's something I want. You're going to give it to me, or else—' He stopped, but the words had purred out of his mouth with a cold terrific deliberation that frightened her more than anything that had yet happened.

White-faced, ashen, she stood against the wall, staring at him. Professor Appleby was lighting a cigarette coolly and deliberately.

'Go to your room,' he said. And then after a significant pause. 'You understand?'

She gasped. And then all at once with a low cry of anguish she turned and darted from the room like a startled fawn.

After she had gone Professor Appleby laughed—his soft, mirthless laugh, and inhaled deeply of his cigarette. He sat down at the piano and played Rubinstein's Melody in F softly, and with the touch of a master. An animal cruelty glowed from his eyes. He felt somehow that tonight the crisis would be reached. He had goaded his wife to the last pitch of desperation; a little more and her taut nerves would snap.

He was not sure that he wanted that. He preferred to play with her a little longer as a cat does with a mouse.

At last, with a little twisted smile on his lips, he rose from the piano, and softly closed the lid.

Treading like a cat he crossed the carpet, opened the door and mounted the stairs. In her room, Eleanor heard his stealthy footsteps along the corridor, and she looked up like a startled fawn. It was he! He was coming as he had said!

Her distress was pitiful, and she was in a state of bodily as well as mental torment; so much so that she was forced to hold her hand to her heart to stay the agony of its wild beating.

The soft footsteps came nearer. A vein throbbed madly in Eleanor Appleby's temple as she crouched back on the bed, and looked up towards the door.

Then she saw his shadow, huge and grotesque, thrown from the illuminated passage into the bedroom, lit only by its tiny reading-lamp. Professor Appleby's face and figure became framed in the doorway. Eleanor felt her senses swooning, and a little cry escaped her.

Professor Appleby laughed softly as his eyes devoured her crouching back on the bed. The light from the passage brought into relief her gleaming white arms and throat, the oval face with its expression of childish anguish. Professor Appleby stretched out a hand from the doorway, and its shadow leapt ahead, and seemed to make with twitching fingers at his wife's throat.

The strain of it on her overwrought nerves was too much, A little shriek left her lips.

Professor Appleby echoed it with a soft laugh.

'Very well, my dear,' he said from the doorway. 'The night is young yet. I will leave you to compose yourself.'

He withdrew, and walked softly down the passage polishing his monocle. This he screwed into his eye with a portentously solemn expression. As a matter of fact, dignity became Professor Appleby very well, and he was able to face the world with a very good countenance. His lapses from dignity were, therefore, all the more shocking, and when the insane light glowed from that heavy, intellectual face it provided a nightmare sight.

He strove to fight his enemy as he descended the stairs. A nerve twitched visibly at his temple. He told himself he was a celebrated figure. The taint of insanity! How ridiculous such a suspicion was in connection with himself! Only the previous day a daily newspaper had published a two-column eulogy on his brilliant research work.

He wrestled with his demons as he descended the stairs. Then all at once he gave a real start as he saw a neat figure in black kneeling at the foot of the stairs, ostensibly brushing the carpet.

Professor Appleby smiled beneath frowning brows. It was Vera. It fed his ego to think that he had paid for the black silk stockings that so enhanced the charm of the house parlour-maid's figure . . . Though he wanted nothing more to do with her now. A scowl darkened on his face as he manœuvred to step past her.

The girl—she was comely, even pretty in a coarse way—looked up at him with a haggard face and a pathetic smile on her lips.

'Sir!'

His momentary anger was gone, and he looked at her indulgently. Indeed for a moment a lambent flame shone in his eyes. She was a trim enough figure in her rather short black frock and white lace apron. Professor Appleby, who had carried on a vulgar intrigue with this woman, and had tired of her—forbidding her, indeed, to come near him, showed a little relenting now for the first time for weeks.

'Well,' he asked softly; 'what is it you want—more money?'

The girl gained courage, and smiled at him coquettishly. She began to believe that she had not lost her hold on him after all, and her visions of what she might expect enlarged correspondingly. She knew that he hated his wife, and, indeed, she had helped him in many a subtle cruelty he had practised upon Eleanor Appleby. And now, tonight that he appeared to be in softer mood, she determined to make a bold bid for him, though secretly she was more than a little afraid of him.

'It's something very important I've got to tell you,' she said, glancing at him archly. 'You've been very cruel to poor little me these last few weeks. I've been afraid, but—oh, you must listen to me. You must.'

Professor Appleby smiled. His glance was like a cold little searchlight playing on her. His curiosity was roused. But she appealed only to his instincts of cruelty now. He had taken his pleasure with her, and she had no longer power to quicken his flaccid interest.

'I shall be in the study,' he said after a long pause. 'Your mistress will not be down again, Vera.'

She nodded dumbly, afraid once more of the sinister side to this man, and Professor Appleby, screwing in his monocle, strolled first into the drawing-room, leaving the door open for a purpose of his own.

With cat-like tread he crossed over to the grand piano, whose sides gleamed sardonically, as if the instrument also enjoyed the cruel jest he contemplated. Lighting a fresh Turkish cigarette, he sat down at the stool, and his fingers caressed the ivory keys. Genius was in his touch, and his voice had uncanny powers of gymnastics. Melody throbbed through the room as he sang and played.

> 'I know not, I care not, where Eden may be,
> But I know
> I'm in very good
> Company.'

He laughed. The old, old song had been one that Eleanor's mother used to sing, and it always brought the tears to his wife's eyes when she heard it. For there is a memory in a song—memory and associations and passionate longing. And from his wife's heart with that song he knew he could wring the bitter, bitter cry: 'Mother, if only you could come back—come back!'

But she had no one in the world. She was merely his possession to do with as he liked.

Upstairs in her room, Eleanor heard the song with its sinister mockery, and something died in her heart for ever. Her pride, her most cherished possession, was beaten to the ground. She was frightened—frightened of being in this big house—frightened of being alone with him.

The tears were rolling down her cheeks, and she made no effort to repress them.

Then, at last, in a panic that he might come again, she climbed off the big downy bed.

Feverishly, desperately, she crossed to the telephone in her room. A silence had fallen in the drawing-room, and she knew her husband's uncanny gift for discovering everything that went on in the house. But she must do it—she must! In a queer, fluttering voice she asked for a number. She hung up the receiver and sat still, the heart of her beating madly. Derek Capel. Queer that she should think of him now. But they had known each other since childhood, and Derek had said when she married that if ever she needed a friend . . .

The telephone bell rang stridently. She stared at it a moment, almost as if she expected an apparition to issue from its mouthpiece. Then with trembling hands she took the receiver again.

Derek Capel's manservant answered the 'phone; and in

answer to her low-voiced inquiry he informed her that his master was not in; he would not be back until later.

She replaced the receiver with a sense of utter, wild desolation. Derek! He was so strong, so self-reliant. She needed someone. After a long moment she went to her writing-table, and feverishly scribbled a note to him.

'Come round . . . some time tonight. Derek, you must. I'm frightened—frightened of him. I've got a feeling that some-thing dreadful is going to happen tonight. My husband has—oh, I cannot tell you. He is a brute. He is not fit to live. If I had the courage I believe I would kill him myself.'

She folded up the letter in haste, and put it in an envelope and addressed it to Derek. If she hurried downstairs now she would catch the gardener, and he would take it and keep silent for a few shillings.

On tiptoe she sped down the stairs, the letter in her hand. The broad staircase turned rather abruptly to face Professor Appleby's study door. She had expected the door to be closed as usual, but as she came round a blaze of light struck her like a blow.

It seemed to Eleanor Appleby then that her heart stopped beating.

For seated at the table with an ugly look on his white face was her husband, and kneeling at his side, pleading with him with tears in her eyes was a woman.

CHAPTER II

THE silence that had fallen a few minutes earlier in the house had been occasioned by the cessation of Professor Appleby's playing, and his strolling into his study next door. He closed the door very carefully, and turned to find Vera, with flushed face, regarding him with an odd light of triumph in her brown eyes.

She crossed to him with a peculiar feline grace that had once attracted him, and placed her arms round his neck.

'My dear—oh, my dear!' she whispered. 'I've wanted to see you alone—oh, so much. And you've kept me at arm's length. You've been so cruel.'

He suffered her caresses, and his vanity was pleased by the mad heaving of her bosom against his shirt front. The girl was evidently distrait. Her eyes were unnaturally bright, and whereas, at their first wooing, she had given herself timidly, fearfully, she now sought for his caresses with wanton eagerness.

Professor Appleby did not at once repulse her: nevertheless there was a cruel glint in his eyes. He had brought her to the dust, and he was fully determined to deal the final blow.

Together they crossed to his desk, and the professor sat down, while she knelt beside him, talking to him excitedly and a little incoherently. Formerly she had been rather like the slave girl who suffers her master's caresses in silence. But now her stress of mind—her very real need—engendered in her a new boldness.

'You do love me a little—just a little?' she said repeatedly. 'Say you do. Hold me in your arms like you used to.'

Professor Appleby sat with broad, stooping shoulders, staring through his monocle, and wondering. It baffled his ingenuity to guess what she wanted from him.

He turned to her at last, and asked her point-blank.

The false gaiety dropped from her, and her hand went up instinctively to her bosom. Now that the crucial moment had come she was afraid. But she had to speak to him—she must.

'It's something very important, sir,' she said, and her voice sounded like a voice in an empty cathedral. 'If you don't help me, I'll—oh, it'll be my ruin.'

Professor Appleby started.

Before he could speak the woman threw her arms around his neck and whispered something. It confirmed the professor's suspicion, and he struggled to throw her arms from him, his face thunderous in its rage.

'What! You dare to tell me it is I, you—you you—' He stopped for a word. Rising to his feet he shook her off, and crossed savagely to the door. 'Get out! Pack your things and get out, you wanton. Don't let me see your face again.'

She faced him, and now she was a virago with flashing eyes and white-streaked face, albeit her voice was pitched low.

'You made me what I am. You! You—no one else! Oh, yes; you pretend not to believe me. But will that doll-faced wife of yours believe? Will the world believe when they see your—'

He turned with a hiss, his hand upraised to check her, his face black as thunder.

She fell to whimpering, awed and frightened by his aspect.

After a pause Professor Appleby crossed to his chair again and slumped into it. The first thunder-struck surprise was giving way to ferocious cruelty. He'd make her suffer for it. She threw herself to her knees and clasped her arms round him, pleading, cajoling, bursting alternately into fresh sobs.

'Won't you—come away with me?' she begged almost in a whisper. 'I'll work for you—slave for you all my life. I'll do what that doll-faced wife of yours could never do; I'll make you love me. It's not money I want, it's—'

He burst into a ferocious laugh at that, and shook her off.

'It's neither that you'll get from me, my dear Vera,' he said in his coldest tones. 'Not a penny piece—nothing, except orders to quit at the end of the week.'

With a terrified gasp she looked at him.

And in his leering eyes she read the truth. He meant it, every word. She struggled to her feet and backed away, staring at him almost fearfully. This was the man to whom she had given herself. And he was as remorseless now in his hatred of her as he had been in his desire.

'You—you can't send me out with nothing,' she whispered.

'I can, and will,' he said in his coldest tone. 'You will leave at the end of the week with a week's wages.'

'But what shall I do?' she gasped. 'I can't face the disgrace, I—' And then suddenly rage transfigured her, and she stamped her foot.

'You monster! You vile brute!' she cried in low, tense tones. 'I'd like to kill you. Oh, if only I could see you die before my eyes now—dying in agonies, I'd be satisfied. Such men as you shouldn't be allowed to live. I—'

Her voice trailed off in a sob. There was a gathering storm in Professor Appleby's eyes that caused her to quail a little. Then all at once he started, fancying he heard a sound in the passage, and holding up his hand to her, he crossed on tip-toe to the door.

As he peered out he fancied he heard a flurry of white disappearing up the staircase. He was not quite certain, and he tiptoed up them, but as he peered in his wife's room he saw that she was in bed and apparently asleep.

Satisfied, he returned.

Down in his study Vera, the house parlourmaid, was glancing around her wildly. She was a little mad. All sorts of thoughts were seething in her head. She hated this man who had betrayed her—hated him with an intensity of feeling that knew no bounds. And in her veins flowed a little gipsy blood. A dangerous mixture. She was not the type of woman to suffer a wrong calmly.

Her eyes espied the medicine cabinet on the right side of the room, and she crossed to it with a rustle of her silk petticoat. There was one bottle on the highest shelf, a little, blue-black bottle marked 'Poison,' and her hand went out to it quickly.

Then she started as she heard Professor Appleby's softly returning footsteps.

When he re-entered the room, she stood at the far end of the room, near the French windows, and near the little round mahogany table that held the professor's wine decanters and a syphon of soda. Professor Appleby had made it a habit of taking a glass of port before retiring to bed.

Vera held her small useless lace apron to her eyes, and her form was shaking with dry, pent-up sobs. But Professor Appleby was in no mood for further hysterics. He crossed to her and grasped her shoulder in a cruel grip.

'Leave this room,' he said in a low voice of menace. She turned with one last defiance, and there was so much deadly earnestness in her tone that it might well have warned Professor Appleby.

'All right; I'm going,' she said stormily. 'I never want to see you again, you monster. But depend upon it, you'll be sorry. You'll be sorry!'

Professor Appleby's lips twitched in a sneering smile as he watched her go with shaking shoulders.

He sat down at his desk again, and for some time engrossed himself in work. He was preparing an important paper to be read at a conference a week hence. But though Professor Appleby did not guess it, forces over which he had no control were shaping to engulf him that night. He was never to read that paper at the medical conference.

Though everything was quiet, save for the ticking of the grandfather clock in Professor Appleby's study, over the house there seemed to hang a brooding threat.

At a distance of little more than five miles away the stately old pile of Capel Manor reared itself against the night sky, its windows lighted and warm with red blinds.

In the drive outside the front door stood a giant Mercedes car, its engine purring almost silently. The owner of the Manor, Derek Capel, had returned home at nearly midnight, after one of his wild and reckless rides through the countryside, but since none of the servants, least of all Derek Capel himself, knew whether he should want the car again, it was left with its engines still running and its headlamps cutting swathes of light through the trees in the drive.

Derek Capel had entered the house briskly, as was his wont, drawing off gloves and coat, with a cheery word for the butler who had opened the door for him, and an ever ready smile on his dark handsome face.

Some people said that Derek Capel was too ready to smile these days. It was as though he were endeavouring to flout cruel Fate who had played so many capricious tricks with him.

Young, handsome, and well endowed with the riches of the world, life should have been pleasant enough for him. And indeed, it could not be said that he did not squeeze every ounce of pleasure from life. His daily and nightly programme was one whirl of gaiety. He was supposed to have attended a society dance in London that night, and he was still in evening dress. But he had long since left the reception hall, and climbed into his car, to drive it recklessly, restlessly through the night.

Women as a rule liked Derek Capel. He was young, eager, and he gave promise of being an ardent lover.

His utter recklessness allied to his jovial laugh and charming manners seemed to the opposite sex to be the concrete of that which is most elusive in life—Romance. And even discerning mothers, who looked upon Derek Capel as an eligible bachelor, did not forget that despite his apparent irresponsibility—say at Brooklands Racing Track, where he was a skilful, as well as a reckless driver—he always managed to emerge triumphant and laughing from his many adventures.

If he dabbled on the Stock Exchange the shares were sure to rise, and Derek Capel was sure to sell out at the right time. He was one of Fortune's favourites.

Yet one would scarce have thought so on seeing him enter the hall of Capel Manor. He handed his hat, gloves and overcoat to the butler with a brisk little nod, but once having dismissed him he stood on the hearthrug fingering his short moustache, and into his face crept a haggard, weary look such as few people had seen there.

'Gad!' he murmured. 'If only I could keep away from the place. If only I could forget!'

That was impossible and he knew it. Life had made of him a spoilt darling—and thwarted him of the one thing he desired above all others. Derek Capel, with a long line of imperious, head-strong ancestors behind him, men who had carved their paths to fame and fortune through all manner of adversities, was not the man to take disappointment lightly.

Indeed, he had taken his blow very hardly indeed.

He strode to the mantelpiece now, and took up a photograph. His dark, handsome eyes were haunted with pain as he gazed at the likeness of Eleanor Appleby.

They had been sweethearts as boy and girl. As he had grown up he had come to love her with that apparently brotherly camraderie that really disguises a very deep-rooted and passionate feeling. He had always understood that one day he should take his bride . . . And then had come the bombshell—her marriage to Professor Appleby.

Derek Capel's teeth showed as a white bar in his tanned face, and for a moment the dancing butterfly of London ball-rooms looked wolfish. 'Curse the fellow!' he raged. 'Heaven knows what fiendish tricks he plays. Oh, I've seen 'em together! If I could only catch him treating her badly—'

It was then that there sounded a knock at the door, and the

butler entered to announce that the gardener at the Lodge had called, and wished to see Mr Capel on a matter of great urgency. He bore a message, he said, from Mrs Appleby.

Derek could hardly restrain his eagerness. He had the aged gardener brought in, and almost snatched the note from him. When he had read it he had looked up, his lips moved voicelessly.

'Come round . . . her husband! . . . Afraid!'

It was on him, too, that strange premonition of disaster, as he stared unseeingly before him for a moment. He was aware that he was trembling a little. His thoughts were like horses out of hand. They galloped away with him. And they were a strange mixture of murderous thoughts, and joyful ones—joyful that Eleanor should have sent to him for aid.

Suddenly he clenched his fists and turned away.

He wanted only a pretext to visit the Lodge, and that was easily supplied. Professor Appleby and he were neighbours, and he often visited there, though he seldom saw Eleanor. They had this much in common, that they both had a love for books, and in particular for rare volumes.

On Derek Capel's last visit, Professor Appleby had expressed a great desire to see a rare first edition of a book on mediæval witchcraft and poisons which he possessed in his library. The younger man had almost forgotten the matter, but now he remembered it again, and thinking it would serve as an excuse for his midnight call, he hurried to get the book.

Snatching hat and coat from the butler, he flung himself recklessly in at the wheel, and sent the long, low Mercedes car travelling through the night like some incredibly swift dragon with its two lighted eyes.

He did not drive the car in through the gates of the Lodge, but drew her to a halt outside and got out with a curiously set face, his dark eyes glowing.

The bare wintry branches of the trees on either side of the drive seemed to stretch out despairing arms to one another as

Derek Capel hastened up the drive. Somewhere an owl hooted dismally, and the sound tore at the man's nerves. To him the house that sheltered Eleanor Appleby seemed a place of queer dread tonight, yet it lured him on, drew him unresistingly as if on a cord.

He rang the front-door bell, and was almost glad to see the bulky figure of Professor Appleby coming himself to answer it.

They kept up an appearance of neighbourly friendship, though Derek Capel was sensible of a latent suspicion, mingled with cunning amusement, in Professor Appleby's eyes at times as he regarded him. The professor seemed delighted to cast Derek Capel and Eleanor together as much as possible, though he was always there to watch them. The younger man had no doubt but that Professor Appleby guessed his secret, and took a malicious enjoyment in taunting him.

Himself, Derek Capel, cherished a flaring hatred for the scientist. It was a hatred that almost frightened him by its violence. He conceived that even if Professor Appleby had not married Eleanor, they were born for mutual dislike. The astonishing part was that he dissembled his real feelings with a cunning that was alien to him. He pretended to a hearty good-fellowship with his neighbour.

. . . And all the time in his heart there was that bitter hatred that went hungry for revenge.

Professor Appleby's white shirt front gleamed at him as the door opened. The great white face with its peculiarly bright eyes dropped the monocle, the eyebrows lifted in surprise, and the lips twitched with their hateful smile.

'Why, it's Capel! Come to give us a look-up on his midnight tear through the country.'

'Frightfully sorry if I'm worrying you,' said Derek Capel hastily. 'I saw the light in your windows, so I thought I'd look in and see whether you were up. Fact is I've been carrying this book you wanted about with me in the car, and it's just occurred to me.'

He held out the book, and his host immediately pounced on it. He turned over its binding, and in a new tone of cordiality invited his midnight guest into the study.

For a moment Professor Appleby was a different man. He was genuinely pleased with the volume Derek Capel had brought him, and he turned its leaves with the delicacy and care of the true bibliophile. It was a rare old volume.

All at once, however, Professor Appleby looked across at his visitor with hooded eyes.

'But Eleanor would be charmed to see you,' he said, with a vague note of mockery. 'I believe she has retired to her room, but I am sure not yet to bed. We will ring and see whether she is disposed to grace our company with her presence.'

And with that twitching smile on his lips he crossed to the bell-push.

Vera, the house parlourmaid, answered the ring, her eyes red from crying. She scowled at her master's urbane request, but vanished without a word. And in a few minutes Eleanor Appleby entered the study.

She came forward, smiling through her fear, and put out a cool little hand to Derek, looking entirely adorable and desirable in her gown of cream ninon and lace. The sight of her set Derek Capel afire, and in his smile and greeting as he took her hand there was a wealth of significance which did not escape the basilisk eyes of Professor Appleby.

Eleanor's heart beat quicker with fear as she looked at her husband. Nothing escaped him. He was smiling now with that twitching of his lips as he looked down at the book, and there was something about his pretence at preoccupation that was very sinister.

'Here it is,' he said suddenly, in his slightly shrill voice. And his interest in the book was now very real. 'It is, as I suspected, made up to my own formula. A poison that leaves no trace. I have it there,' he went on in some excitement, pointing to the chemical cabinet. 'You see!—In that little blue bottle! I have not experimented with it yet, but I am almost assured that it will prove to be what I claim.'

Involuntarily Eleanor Portal and Derek Capel exchanged glances.

Impelled by a fascination she could not understand or resist, Eleanor crossed to the medicine chest and reached out a delicate hand for the little blue-black bottle labelled 'Poison,' which stood there, and at which the professor had pointed.

Revulsion and attraction were pulling different ways with her. She had a shuddering impulse to throw up her arm across her forehead, to shield her gaze from that impish black bottle. And yet another thought came into her brain. If the worst came to the worst it would be—useful!

Professor Appleby was watching the play of emotion on her face closely, and suddenly as she was about to take the bottle he shot out an arm and grasped her wrist.

'I don't think,' he said curtly, 'that we'll allow you to try any experiments with that bottle. They might have unfortunate results.'

She dropped her gaze, trembling violently.

Professor Appleby was, indeed, in one of his queer moods tonight, and electric tension hung in the air. But he was all urbanity as he turned once more to Derek Capel.

'You must have a spot of something, old fellow, after your drive. What is it to be? Whisky, eh?'

'Just a finger,' agreed Derek nonchalantly.

But directly the professor's back was turned to go for the drinks, Derek's dark, handsome eyes sought and met Eleanor's. He asked questions barely in a whisper. What happened? Had he ill-treated her? How could he help?

Impulsively Derek's hand went out and found that of the woman he loved. She did not resist. Indeed, she clung to it. She was scarcely conscious of what she did; only knew that her heart was breaking with sorrow—and that Derek Capel was a very dear and old friend.

It was then, as they stood intimately near to one another,

that Professor Appleby glanced in the mirror hanging against the wall—a mirror that reflected them both. A terrible savagery fleeted across his features, and there was a flash like summer lightning in his eyes.

He had suspected it. But the actual proof roused the raging beast in him.

He turned, and like a hawk from the wrist of the hunter, struck across the room, and seized his wife's wrist in a grip of iron. She cried out at the pain of his grip, but he was brutally savage now, his thick underlip protruding as he thrust her towards the door.

'Another lover, eh?' he hissed as he pushed her past the curtains. 'I'll attend to him. Get up to your room.'

He watched her as she staggered rather than walked up the staircase, her slim shoulders shaking. At length, moistening his dry lips with the tip of his tongue, he strode back to the study.

Derek Capel was still there, standing near the shaded lamp. His arms were folded, and he appeared to be quite dispassionate. Professor Appleby, a monstrous glowering figure, came forward to the desk, and peered at him for a long moment as a mastiff might peer at a pup.

Derek Capel, faintly amused, returned his glance steadily and disdainfully.

At last Professor Appleby took up his wine glass, but paused to make remark.

'Generally I would feel inclined to snap a man's spine if he paid too much attention to my wife. But in this case it's Eleanor who will pay.' He rocked back on his heels with a tinny cackle. 'You fool, Capel, you love her—but she's mine. And tonight she'll pay—pay—pay!'

Derek Capel snapped open his cigarette case, and lit one of the white tubes with a hand that was a trifle unsteady. The blue smoke streamed from his nostrils as he silently consumed the cigarette. He evidently badly needed the sedative. But he would not touch the whisky that had been poured out for him.

At last with his upper lip lifting in what was almost a silent snarl, he reached for his coat and hat, and slung the former over his arm, strolling towards the door. On the threshold he turned. 'You cur, Appleby,' he said, very quietly and contemptuously. 'You cur! You're not fit to have the care of a woman. I feel that you're vile—one of the vilest things God made. Be very careful that it is not you who pays!'

He turned and strode from the room and the house, while Professor Appleby stared after him in gibbering rage.

'My God!' burst from the professor's lips.

He seemed on the verge of apoplexy, and staggered towards a chair, sinking into it heavily. But after a time he became more calm, though it was a sinister calm.

A silence fell on the house, save for the ticking of the clock.

If Derek Capel wished to incite the professor to murder he could scarcely have gone about it in a more efficacious manner. With his heavy-lidded eyes bent on the ground Professor Appleby sat brooding.

His thoughts were all of the white, soft woman lying upstairs in bed, with the heart of her beating madly. He clenched and unclenched his hands, and at last got up and paced up and down the study. He saw the glass of port he had poured out, and lifting it, drained it off at a gulp.

A minute ticked away.

Heavens, what was it? He felt queer—bad! All at once he commenced panting hoarsely—breathing with difficulty. His head felt as if it were charged with cotton-wool on fire, and in his stomach was an awful pain.

Madly he tore at his collar, wrenched it from his neck. He could not breathe. Like a drunkard lurching towards an objective, he lurched towards an arm-chair. He wanted to cry out—to call for help, but he could not. His agony was immense, but mercifully it was short-lived. The death-rattle was already in his throat, and all was going black before him.

He fell heavily into the chair, and in doing so knocked a

costly old Chinese vase from a pedestal nearby. It crashed just outside the fringe of the carpet in a thousand pieces—and the sound of it was like the last trump in that expectant house of dread. From the bedroom above came cries of alarm, and mingling with them were the terrible sobs that tore the throat of Professor Appleby in his last, short death agonies.

Eleanor Appleby in dressing-gown and slippers rushed into the room, followed by two frightened maids in their night attire, the old cook and housekeeper, who had managed Professor Appleby's menage for a generation, and Vera, the house parlour-maid, who alone seemed to remain calm.

'Why—what—good heavens!' Eleanor exclaimed, staring with dilated eyes at the huddled figure of her husband in the arm-chair.

He managed to turn to her with glazed eyes half-opened, and dying, his hatred stabbed at her from those eyes.

'I've been poisoned,' he whispered hoarsely. 'Poisoned by—by—' his eyes wandered round the room, and fixed Vera and then Derek Capel, who had entered quietly.

He subsided in the arm-chair, his last breath spent in that accusation.

There was a pregnant pause, filled with the gasps of those in the room. The servants, for the most part, were petrified with fear. The old cook could not even wail. She was sucking in breath like a fish out of water, her ample bosom heaving spasmodically. Amongst the servants only Vera, the parlour-maid, remained calm, and there was a contemptuous curl to her lips that could hardly be deemed respectful in the presence of death.

Eleanor was trembling violently, and her childish face was pitiful.

'Derek—hold me,' she whispered. 'I—I feel I'm going to faint.'

There were tiny beads of perspiration on Derek Capel's brow. His face was pale beneath his tan, and quivering as he put an arm round her. He was hardly more collected than she, but he appeared to make a great effort.

'It's a great shock,' he said in a low tone. 'Er—if you'll excuse me, I think I'll have a spot of something to pull me together.'

He made a movement towards the round mahogany table, and took up the port decanter. But as he did so his hand shook violently, and in his eyes—studiously averted from the decanter he had picked up—there was a look of stark fear.

Eleanor bit her white lips. She could have cried out as she saw him take out the stopper. He was pouring the liquid in a glass with a shaking hand that spilled a little of it on the carpet. And Vera, the house parlourmaid, was watching the procedure through narrowed lids.

Suddenly Eleanor Appleby's body springs were released. With a little cry, half moan, she darted forward and took the decanter from him. He yielded it to her grasp like a child, and looked at her stupidly as she tried to smile at him—a twisted, agonised little smile that struggled like the sun against the clouds.

'Don't, Derek,' she whispered. 'Not that. You—I'm going to play the game through to the end.'

She seemed on the verge of fainting. And then all of a sudden she gave a little gasp.

'Oh!'

There was a sound of a crash. The decanter had slipped from her nerveless fingers, and now it lay on the floor, its glass shattered in pieces, and the red port streamed over the carpet in a blood-like pool.

A silence fell.

Eleanor moved across the room with faltering steps, and then suddenly threw up her arms like a baffled swimmer and nearly collapsed on the floor. Just in time, however, the old gardener, George—he who had taken her message to Derek Capel that night—dashed forward from the curtained doorway and caught her, leading her to a chair.

There she lay inertly, her hands covering her face and short dry gasps coming from her lips. Her fair hair had become loose and flowed over her shoulders, enveloping her like a cloud.

Derek Capel had made no move to help her. He stared down at the red pool on the floor, and something like a sigh was forced from his lips. He set down the glass at length, which contained merely enough dregs to cover the bottom.

'Well, we'd better 'phone the police, I suppose,' he said, with a dry rattle in his throat.

His dark, strangely handsome face working convulsively he crossed to the telephone in the hall. In a few moments he was in communication with the local police station and giving them particulars of what had happened.

All this time, Vera, the house parlourmaid, was regarding her mistress with a curious intentness. A tiny smile twitched scornfully on her lips, and once or twice she nodded slightly as one who should say: 'I know something about this, and I mean to tell it.'

Vera, indeed, was amazingly self-possessed for one who saw her illicit lover lying huddled in a chair with death's cold touch upon his face. A lover, moreover, from whom she had expected certain things, and who had betrayed and spurned her. She might scarce have been expected to weep, yet a little natural agitation would not have been incongruous to the occasion.

And so the police found them when they arrived scarcely more than five minutes later at the Lodge. Chief Inspector Brent of the C.I.D. of Scotland Yard, whose home happened to be in this quiet Sussex village, had been at the local police station when the late night call came through, and so the case had the attention of one of the most alert and keenly analytical criminal brains in the country right from the commencement.

Chief Inspector Brent was one who never placed too great a discount on first impressions. As he strode into the study his narrowed eyes took in every detail of the tableau, and noted all the persons in it, their position and demeanour.

The two maidservants, exhausted from hysterical weeping, but still too frightened to come directly into the study, were hanging back with the old housekeeper behind the curtains that, half-drawn, separated the study from the hall. The old gardener, George, was with them, stolid as ever, but with a hint of defiance in his seamed face.

Chief Inspector Brent glanced at them, then at Vera, whose general air was one of suppressed excitement, triumph and malice. Her eyes were very bright, and malice was very apparent in them as she looked from the detective to her mistress.

Inspector Brent ruled out all the servants as being of little consequence in the matter, except Vera.

His swift survey of the scene stopped at Derek Capel, who had now assumed a nonchalant attitude, and was smoking a cigarette. 'You rang up the station, sir,' he said, rather as if stating a fact than asking a question.

Derek Capel nodded. 'Yes,' he replied. 'As you see, Professor Appleby has died—suddenly. It seemed to me to be a matter for the police.'

'Quite right,' said the inspector, smiling ironically and twisting his heavy moustache. 'Ah, what's that?' he exclaimed. And as if noticing it for the first time, he crossed to the broken decanter and knelt beside the pool of wine on the carpet.

There was a queer tension—a silence. Every one except Eleanor Appleby craned forward as if noticing it, too, for the first time. That tell-tale decanter quite obviously contained the key to the riddle of Professor Appleby's death.

'I imagine that the professor was taking his nightcap of port when he—er—collapsed,' Derek Capel said in a voice that sounded ragged somehow.

Inspector Brent slewed his head round to look at him, his face very keen.

'The assumption being that he had some kind of fit, eh?' he drawled, jerking erect. 'Yes; that seems to fit the case.' He took out his notebook, making entries and glancing at the professor, whose disordered hair and collar torn from the stud were eloquent of his death agonies; from the professor he looked repeatedly down at the broken decanter and the pool of wine that stained the carpet. Whatever his deductions may have been—and we can assume that Chief Inspector Brent was no fool—there was one in the room who was determined that he should not for a moment form a wrong impression as to how the decanter had been broken.

Vera plucked at his sleeve. The flags of colour had mounted to her cheeks, and her bosom was heaving madly. Her voice had acquired a shrill breathlessness.

'He didn't drop it himself—the professor. It was she that done it'—her finger flung out like a taunt, pointing at Eleanor, who looked like a weeping goddess in the arm-chair. 'Yes, she broke the decanter and spilt the wine,' concluded Vera with intense malice.

Chief Inspector Brent twirled his moustache and looked across at Professor Appleby's wife. And a painful silence fell.

CHAPTER III

IT was broken by the arrival of Doctor Alec Portal—for Capel had rung him up immediately after concluding his message to the police station. Doctor Portal came into the study with his bag, which he immediately set down on the table. As he drew off his gloves he looked round upon the study and its occupants, but without saying a word.

His brows were drawn, however, giving his face a hawk-like expression. He crossed over to the chair, and but a momentary examination of the dead man sufficed. He dropped a limp hand into Professor Appleby's lap as he straightened himself.

'There's nothing we can do, of course,' he said quietly as he looked over at Inspector Brent. 'The cause of the death will have to be decided by post-mortem examination. His own doctor will attend to say whether he was subject to fits or not.'

'Fits be hanged!' exclaimed Inspector Brent in a quite unprofessional outburst. 'He died when he was taking his drink before retiring. There appear to be strange circumstances in this case, and I am afraid I must detain the company present while I ask questions of each.'

Chief Inspector Brent himself could not have explained what had jolted him out of his usual suave manner. But he almost glared at the doctor, who for his part confronted him with clean-cut face, very set, and eyes narrowed to shining slits. No doubt the atmosphere in the room was very tense—electric with excitement—and in such an atmosphere mental telepathy exercises its uncanny workings. Chief Inspector Brent had already decided that he had a line of investigation to follow, and it would entail a rather lengthy and no doubt painful interrogation of Eleanor Appleby.

Doctor Alec Portal guessed all this. He knew what was in

the Yard man's thoughts, and he was aflame with anger. He happened to know more of the affairs of this strange house than did Inspector Brent—he knew, for instance, that Professor Appleby had been very, very near the borderline of insanity, and that he was just the man to kill himself. But murder! That was a terrible word to use in connection with the beautiful girl-wife who sat tortured in the chair.

With her fair hair loose, and her dressing-gown scarce concealing her beautifully moulded figure under the frothy, lacy night-gown, she stirred his senses oddly even then.

'I don't think it would be wise to detain Mrs Appleby tonight,' the doctor said stiffly. 'As her medical adviser I have been in attendance upon her, and I know that she is in a considerably overwrought state. Tonight's events may bring a climax unless she has rest. She can make a statement if she cares, but I must object to any form of Third Degree.'

The distinguished Yard chief looked at him sharply and resentfully.

'A very ill-considered remark, doctor,' he said sternly. 'You may, on reflection, care to withdraw it.'

Doctor Portal bowed.

'I withdraw and apologise,' he said awkwardly. 'Nevertheless this lady has been near to a nervous breakdown for some time, and I must beg of you to consider her feelings as much as possible. She has suffered a great deal.'

Thus did the two men range themselves on opposite sides. Alec Portal, deeply chivalrous and in love, scorned the very idea of foul play in connection with the professor's death. And that the breath of suspicion should for an instant be directed against the fair and gracious girl, who had suffered so much during Professor Appleby's lifetime, and had borne it with quiet dignity and womanly resignation, was unbelievable, monstrous!

For two years she had been chained by the marriage tie to this human fiend. She had endeavoured to preserve a brave front to the world, and to bolster up the illusion that she was happily married to a sane and normal man, who cherished and loved her as a man should cherish and love the woman he takes for a wife. All that Eleanor Appleby had done, as much for the professor's sake as her own. But he had openly flouted her and insulted her in public. He had shown that he regarded her as one of the smallest and meanest of his goods and chattels, and he had shown, too, on more than one occasion the subtle, hideous cruelty to which he constantly subjected this beautiful girl wife of his.

. . . There had been the occasion of the local flower show, when Eleanor had appeared at Professor Appleby's side, a fairylike breathless creature in a white, girlish frock with short sleeves. The villagers had openly admired Professor Appleby's girl bride, her beauty and sweet modesty. Perhaps, as locals will, they gaped too much. But it was more likely that Professor Appleby, with his subtle, fiendish cruelty, had deliberately intended to humiliate his wife when, before the officials of the flower show, he icily informed Eleanor that she was not modestly dressed and ordered, her to go home.

The frock had been ravishingly perfect in its white modesty and sweet simplicity. Doctor Alec Portal recalled the incident vividly, and also his own indignation at the slight that had been put upon one who had appeared so gracious and ideal a wife for any man. Perhaps that had been the beginning of his interest in Eleanor Appleby.

It had grown unconsciously since he had attended her as medical adviser. His heart had ached to see the brave way she had tried to bear up under her husband's persistent cruelty. And he had grown more and more alarmed to find that Eleanor was being tortured beyond all endurance, that she was becoming listless, pale, but a shadow of her former radiant self.

Finally had come the alarming discovery that she was very near to nervous prostration. Then Doctor Alec Portal's protective instincts had reared up, and he had become emboldened to speak candidly and straightforwardly to her husband.

With the result that he had been ordered from the house. And on going he had made the great discovery that he loved Eleanor Appleby—another man's wife!

And now this! The dead man lying there huddled in the chair, with his head hanging curiously to one side. And Eleanor Appleby was free! Doctor Alec Portal hardly understood the chaos of his own emotions, yet he knew as he looked into the hard, sardonic eyes of Chief Inspector Brent, of Scotland Yard, that, come what might, he would fight for the woman he loved, protect her from the harshness and injustice of the world, and, if he were allowed to do so, make up to her a little of what she had lost.

Chief Inspector Brent, for his part, was in his most judicial mood. He had seen too many women in distress to be affected by the sight of this beautiful, overwrought and forlorn girl now. As he often maintained, he merely wished to get at the truth.

He approached Eleanor now, tapping his notebook with his pencil.

'Madam,' he asked in hard, even tones, 'can you throw any light upon this matter? If so, I should be glad if you would assist me as much as possible. Kindly look at the deceased. Was he, in life, your husband. Professor Appleby?'

Eleanor started up. Cold horror transfigured her beautiful oval face. She hardly knew what she was saying. She had been through so much, and now the snapping point was almost reached.

'No, no! I can't look! It is too terrible! He was a monster—a fiend! Oh, he deserved to die!'

'There is a latin tag, *moriotorium nil nisi bonum*,' said the inspector gravely, compressing his lips. 'No doubt you know it. It means "of the dead let nothing but good be spoken". You were afraid of your husband then—'

'He—he had been so cruel!' gasped Eleanor. 'He was in one of his worst moods tonight—'

At this stage Doctor Alec Portal stepped forward determinedly, his blue eyes holding a savage gleam.

'I can't allow any more of this, inspector,' he said harshly. My patient must have rest and care and attention at once, otherwise I shall not answer for the consequences. Besides, this cross-examination is irregular. If I were Mrs Appleby, I should insist that my lawyer were present before answering any more questions.'

Their eyes met in an angry rapier play duel once again.

'It is within my province to ask Mrs Appleby what she knows of this affair,' the detective said coldly. 'Of course, if she prefers not to make any voluntary statement—'

Once again he looked directly at Eleanor, who was supported in Alec Portal's arms, her whole body shaken with silent, tear-less sobs. She wanted to run away somewhere and sob, sob, until her heart broke. She turned to Inspector Brent, eyes asking for compassion, lashes tremulous, lips a-quiver. But in his cold gray eyes was only a relentless inquiry and suspicion.

The blood mantled her face like a flame, and she made a clutch at her reeling senses.

'What is it you want to know?' she asked in a low, proud voice.

'I have only one or two questions,' answered the detective. 'Firstly, how did you discover your husband's death?'

'I—I heard the vase smash,' she answered, 'It must have wakened me, for I was in bed. Then I heard groans and cries and I came rushing downstairs, to discover—this.'

'Thank you.' The detective bowed slightly. 'The vase was broken when you arrived on the scene then. And the port decanter?'—he raised his eyebrows slightly as he said this.

Involuntarily Eleanor's beautiful brown eyes took a startled look, a gasp left her white lips, and she looked quickly across at Derek Capel, who smiled and nodded reassurance.

'I—I don't know,' she made answer, 'Everything is so confused. I—I moved near him to look, and—I think there was another crash.' She threw up her white arm across her temples, a sickening horror upon her all of a sudden. 'Oh, I must get away from this room—I can't stay here any longer.'

Inspector Brent nodded his gray head. 'Very well. That will be all for tonight, Mrs Appleby, thank you. Doubtless at a later date you will remember exactly what happened—whether you brushed against the table in your agitation and knocked over the wine decanter. In any case the spilt wine will be analysed.'— he looked keenly at her as he said this.

But if she heard the words and understood their hidden imputation, she showed only vast relief at being dismissed, and turned away, a pathetic, forlorn figure, with Alec Portal's arm around her shoulder.

As she went up the stairs, with the old housekeeper following eagerly to render her youug mistress any attention she might require, Chief Inspector Brent turned and looked with a significant expression on his grizzled face through the open doorway into the hall, where, with two policemen, stood a plain-clothes officer making notes.

It was evident that Chief Inspector Brent had made up his mind already as to the facts of the case. He was noted for these quick decisions, on which he based his lines of investigation. And almost invariably his first considered opinion on a case proved to be the right one.

In this case he took the strong view that Professor Appleby had been poisoned, and that his wife, Eleanor Appleby, should answer to the charge of having caused his death. When he made up his mind as to who was the culprit Inspector Brent always pursued the case with a relentless vigour and tenacity of purpose that, in most cases, earned him success and proved the guilt of the person suspected.

After Eleanor Appleby had retired to her room, the police investigations assumed a brisk and more normal form. There was a touch of the gruesome when an ambulance arrived, and the mortal remains of Professor Appleby, brilliant and eccentric scientist, were removed. The newspaper reporters by now had arrived, and were flocking round the house like vultures on a stricken field. There would be a sensational tit-bit of

news to place on the breakfast table of the great British public
on the morrow.

SUDDEN DEATH OF BRILLIANT
SCIENTIST!
PROFESSOR APPLEBY DIES IN A FIT.
STRONG SUSPICION OF FOUL PLAY.

Doctor Alec Portal visualised all this and his face was grave
as he waited in the ante-room with the servants, each of whom
was to be questioned in turn by Inspector Brent, who was even
then in the drawing-room interrogating Derek Capel.

Doctor Portal was determined to give his evidence with
decision at the inquest, and he felt sure that it would carry
weight. He scorned the idea of foul play. Such things only
happened as a rule in sensational plays. He fully concurred in
the view that Professor Appleby had met a violent end, but it
was violence that was engendered by his own uneasy brain and
turbulent nature. In a word, he had died from an apoplectic fit,
and medical examination would no doubt bear out this view.

What then was the police inspector from Scotland Yard
making all this ridiculous fuss about?

In the drawing-room Inspector Brent sat at a table with his
plain-clothes sergeant at a smaller table behind him to take
notes, and facing them, lounging in an easy chair, was Derek
Capel.

He was superbly at his ease now. The dark, handsome eyes
were mocking, the tips of his tiny black moustache were curled,
and his face was as fresh and debonair as if he had just risen
in the morning.

'You say you did not see Mrs Appleby drop the decanter?'
Inspector Brent asked gravely.

'Not a bit of it,' answered Derek Capel, crossing his legs
easily. 'What would she be wanting with a decanter when she'd
just seen her husband dead?'

Chief Inspector Brent leant over his desk. 'You are not shielding anyone, Mr Capel?' he asked, his shaggy brows knit.

Derek Capel laughed. But there was a haunted look deep in his eyes. 'I see you disdain finesse, inspector,' he said. 'No; I am not shielding Mrs Appleby.'

'Yet you were very good friends,' pursued the inspector. 'You say you came here tonight to lend Professor Appleby a book? You saw Mrs Appleby, who retired to her room ten minutes or quarter of an hour before you left. Did you part or good terms with the professor?'

'Most certainly,' exclaimed Derek Capel, raising his eyebrows.

'Were there any signs of a quarrel of anything like that then?'

'I don't suggest there was a *struggle*,' the detective said, tapping his pencil on the desk, 'but you may have left rather hurriedly. For you see, Mr Capel, there was a glass of whisky left on the desk, evidently poured out for someone.'

Derek Capel smiled.

'It was poured out for Mrs Appleby,' he said easily. 'She left it, pleading a headache, and retired to her room. I myself drank port. You will no doubt find two glasses with traces of port in them if you search diligently.'

'But Mrs Appleby never drinks whisky,' the inspector said, leaning forward again. 'I have ascertained that from the house parlourmaid, who persists in her statement that she saw Mrs Appleby drop the port decanter.'

Derek Capel laughed contemptuously. 'I cannot answer for the testimony that Vera, the parlourmaid, gives,' he rejoined. 'Probably Mrs Appleby does not drink whisky, and that was why she refused it. I see no mystery in that.'

'You are shielding her, Mr Capel,' the detective said sharply. 'Now tell me this: why did you return to the house at all?'

'I heard screams and cries, I—'

'But you should have driven well away by then,' pursued the detective relentlessly. 'Is it not the truth, Mr Capel, that you are often to be seen in the vicinity of the Lodge. You hang about here in your car. You are, in fact, in love with Mrs Appleby, and even after you had left the house you could not tear yourself away.'

Derek Capel threw back his head with a joyous chuckle.

'So that's the gossip of the village, eh? You have been talking to the servants, inspector—especially Vera, I suppose. Take it from me it is all a pack of lies. If I suffer from insomnia and do ride round o' nights, am I to be accused of haunting the house of another man's wife?'

Chief Inspector Brent rose impatiently. He was evidently finished with Derek Capel, and was more convinced than ever that Mrs Appleby had poisoned her husband.

'One last question, and you may go,' he said harshly. 'You finished your port, and Professor Appleby finished his, and he saw you to the door, eh?'

'That is so,' answered the other with a mocking light in his eyes.

'Then, in your opinion would Mrs Appleby have had time to reach the decanter whilst the professor was seeing you off at the door?' He thumped on the table emphatically as he saw a startled look jump to Derek Capel's eyes. 'Ah, I thought so! That is your opinion of what happened. The professor came back, had another glass of port—and died!'

'It is all rubbish,' said Derek Capel harshly, and he had gone pale as death now. 'She is good and pure. She would not do such a thing, though God knows she had enough provocation. Poisoning is an art of foreigners, and—'

'I think that is all, Mr Capel,' the inspector said, suddenly suave and calm. 'Go out by that door, if you please.'

After he had gone the inspector had the servants in one by one, except Vera, whom he had already questioned. The two servants declared positively that they had not seen Mrs Appleby drop the decanter and break it, but then they had been standing all the time outside the door, and the curtain had screened their mistress from their view. They had heard a crash.

George, the aged gardener at the Lodge, yielded a complete

blank. His stupid answers to every question confirmed the inspector in the opinion that he was half-witted. If only he had known! George, the gardener, could have told a strange story of what had taken place at the Lodge that night. He could have told terrible stories of Professor Appleby's cruelty, his fits of insanity, for George, the oldest retainer of the house, had suffered more during the years through the mad genius of his master than anyone. Perhaps that was why he had the silence of the sphinx in his tongue.

Mary, the old housekeeper, too, was incoherent and babbling. Her tale was not worth a fig to the inspector. She seemed more concerned about having 'a beautiful funeral for the pore master' now than anything else.

It was the inspector's view that the testimony of servants was never worth much. They were generally illiterate and of a low order of intelligence, and could be made to believe and corroborate anything so long as it was impressed strongly enough upon them that it had happened. And this is a view that both the bar and the bench generally recognise as having a very sound basis.

But Vera! She was not of the ordinary type. A voluptuous, wanton creature of unbridled passions, she played some strange part in this drama which the man from Scotland Yard could not quite fathom. Her intelligence was quite up to standard. And it was commensurate with her malicious hatred of her beautiful mistress.

A lingering doubt remained in Inspector Brent's mind as he prepared his notes in the early hours of that morning.

Why did one woman ever hate another? Was it not often because of rivalry for the affections of a man? Then—

With an impatient gesture Chief Inspector Brent of Scotland Yard dismissed that line of thought as likely to lead nowhere. He rose from the desk and crossed over to the medicine cabinet in Professor Appleby's study. It was the small blue-black bottle marked poison that immediately riveted his attention.

Inspector Brent did not touch it. But he decided to have it examined for finger marks. In the pursuance of his duty the Yard chief was a conscientious and thoroughgoing man. That was how he got his results.

Upstairs in her little pink and white bedroom Eleanor Appleby lay very still, with the heart of her beating madly in the big downy bed. Once she started up wildly with a great fear upon her. In the darkness she had envisioned her husband's white, gross face, with the glittering eyes of insanity, the gleaming monocle in the right eye, and the tight, red mouth twisted in a crooked smile.

'Oh . . . Oh . . . Goodness!'

The words came from her in a gasp. That red mouth twisted in a more crooked smile upon her—it was like a red wound in his white face! The eyes gleamed malevolently; the white face seemed to loom nearer her.

She beat at the vision with little fluttering hands, gasping and crying. 'I didn't do it—I didn't do it!' she cried huskily. 'I—oh, I don't know who did it! Don't ask me!'

And then the vision was gone.

She sank down on the pillow again, palpitant, overwhelmed with horror, and it was a long time before the mad beating of her heart commenced to subside. He was haunting her! Her whole being was racked by pain and anguish and half-stifled sobs.

She had seen him! He was haunting her! What did he want from her—the truth? Dear Heaven bear witness that she had not poisoned him. She had not taken any part in it.

Then all at once the kaleidoscopic images in her reeling brain—images of her husband, smiling crookedly at her, of Derek, with his haunting, dark eyes; the detective, threatening and stern—all these vanished, and into her brain came one awful thought. With her own hands she had touched the poison bottle in the cabinet! She remembered that, remembered the dreadful thoughts that had been in her mind at the time.

What else had she done? Surely there was no hiatus in her brain, no blank in her living memory of that evening! Dear Heaven! Surely she had not done this thing! She started up in a frenzy, her eyes full of horror, staring into the opaque blackness of the room. No, God!—oh, no, it was not true! No—no!

For answer she seemed to hear her husband's jeering laugh; Professor Appleby's voice through the darkness, like the croaking of Stygian frogs, telling her that it was so—that she was the murderess.

She could stand it no longer. She must escape somehow—somewhere from this house of horror and dread. She slipped out of bed, an ethereal figure in her nightgown, and crammed her feet into a pair of satin slippers, then hastily crossed over to her wardrobe.

From it she flung everything—Paris gowns and frocks that billowed on the floor in a frothy mass of delicate colours. With her large brown eyes dilated unnaturally in her delicately moulded face, her fair hair tumbled in a gossamer cloud around her shoulders, she presented a wonderful phantasy for an artist—a phantasy of fear. Often she glanced behind her in childish fear, but there was no one now save herself in the room; the visions no longer haunted her.

At length she found what she sought, a tweed costume for golfing or walking. She dressed hastily, feverishly, and then, a slim, girlish figure in the tweed suit, she crossed to the bed and pulling off the bedclothes commenced to knot them together to form an improvised rope.

She had done this years before when as a girl at a boarding-school she had planned with other girls to escape from the dormitory on some madcap prank. It had worked successfully then; the rope sheet tied to the bed post. She prayed that it might do so now.

At length her work was done, and she pushed the bed on

its castors over to the window. The first pale streaks of dawn were appearing in the sky, and in the leaden, cold half-light of the heavens there seemed to Eleanor Appleby to hover a brooding threat.

Yet she must escape. To stay here any longer would be intolerable. Giving herself no time to think of the madness of her act, she tied the bed sheet securely to the bed, and furling the rest out of the window she climbed on to the window sill.

She commenced to lower herself inch by inch. It was nearly twenty feet to the ground. All at once she felt faint, dizzy. Her heart was beating as if to stifle her. She had a wild impulse to let go, to fall to the ground and so end it all. But even in the most desperate of God's creatures there is a tenacious clinging to life, and though she dared not look down, she continued to lower herself to the ground, mastering her giddiness and faint-ness with a great effort.

At long last she touched terra firma, and like a startled fawn, she darted away, leaving the tell-tale white sheet hanging from the window. She was keeping close to the ivy and lichen-covered wall, in the shadows, hoping against hope that her wild ruse would avail her, and that she would succeed in escaping from this house where she had spent so many months of misery and terror which had culminated at last in tragedy.

She knew her way well, and was making for the tree-shadowed drive, the gates and liberty, when all at once she almost collided with the figure of a man that appeared from the bushes right in her path.

'Eleanor! Oh, my dear!'

She started violently and stopped dead. She could only stare at him, trembling as a child would do on the sudden break of a storm.

At last she found her voice.

'Derek!' she whispered. 'Oh, you gave me such a fright! I—I thought— Is it really you.'

It was Derek Capel smiling at her through the darkness, and

in his most devil-may-care and reckless mood. It seemed to Eleanor all at once that he was the only real person in all this nightmare world of horror. Yes, it was the same handsome, dissolute face, with the tiny pointed moustache on the curved upper lip, the same clear-cut features, with the fine chin dimpled in the centre, denoting the violent, passionate nature of the man; and the same dark, smiling eyes that could speak more eloquently of the things this man desired to tell this woman than could Derek Capel with his own lips.

'Eleanor! Little woman,' he said huskily, approaching a step nearer. 'I've been watching your window. I saw you escape. I—I've been making the same plans as a matter of fact. Let's steal away together, little one. Just you and I, to a new world where no one knows us, where no one will ever guess. I've made all the plans. I've arranged false passports, and with a swift dash to the coast we can get away before dawn.'

Eleanor's heart was beating to suffocation. Here was a way of escape. She could not deny to herself the truth: Derek Capel worshipped her, adored her. He would commit any mad, reckless act for her sake.

Yet if she took this love he offered her now—this protection and help, what would happen? Sooner or later—very soon, perhaps—the police would find her. Their suspicions would be strengthened by the fact that she had run away from this horror that had come into her life.

As she stood there, swaying on her decision, her mind in a whirl, Eleanor Appleby had a sudden tingling of fear, all her instincts rearing in warning. And she looked around her fearfully.

She could perceive nothing in the darkness, and she returned her gaze with half-parted lips to handsome, reckless Derek whom she had known as a boy, and who now offered to become her lover.

He was so preoccupied that no sixth sense served to warn him. Yet, actually, Chief Inspector Brent of Scotland Yard with three of his men had crept up very close behind the bushes, and the Yard chief was only waiting before pouncing and making his coup, to see if the woman he was convinced had killed Professor Appleby would yet convict herself from her own lips.

'I can't go with you, Derek,' she whispered with trembling lips. 'I—I can't let you share this trouble. It is good of you—noble. But—'

With a sudden exclamation Derek Capel slipped an arm round her shoulders and drew her to him. His arms tightened, and he held her close. She felt the mad beating of his heart, and curiously enough her own became numbed by an icy feeling of despair.

She shivered a little in his arms. 'Eleanor,' he whispered, 'you are mine—mine! I won you, d'you hear? Don't be afraid,' he went on, as though speaking to a child. 'I'll take you away from all this—where we shall be safe. Eleanor, you know I love you—you beautiful, tantalising little thing. I'd go through hell for you. Kiss me, sweetheart—kiss me, and make me the happiest man in the world, before we go away and leave it all—'

He broke off suddenly in utter consternation. 'God!' he jerked out. He was looking around him like a hunted animal.

In an access of panic Eleanor freed herself from his grasp. For she had seen, too, now. In ungovernable alarm and fear she found herself staring at Chief Inspector Brent of Scotland Yard, who stood before her grimly, with three uniformed police constables behind him.

'I am sorry you should resort to the expedient of climbing out of the window of your bedroom, madam,' said the Yard man gruffly. 'It makes it necessary for me to take a certain course.'

He was evidently ill at ease, and for a moment there was a tense silence.

'You know me,' he went on. 'I am Chief Inspector Brent of New Scotland Yard. You are Eleanor Appleby. And I am afraid I must detain you in custody on suspicion of being concerned in the death of Professor Appleby, your husband. I should like to deal with you as gently as possible. Better come quietly with me to the station, and I must warn you that anything you say may be used in weight of evidence against you.'

There was a hoarse, enraged shout from Derek, who moved galvanically, like a madman. He was quickly pinioned, however, by a burly police sergeant.

And in that moment Eleanor's terror-stricken eyes swept wildly round. The full horror of the situation was breaking on her. She was to be arrested—accused of murder!

A cry of sheer terror broke from her lips, and she swayed dizzily.

Two policemen moved forward quickly, and caught her as she collapsed in a dead faint.

CHAPTER IV

WHEN Eleanor came back to consciousness it was to find herself in almost complete darkness.

She sat up with a start, her heart beating wildly. She was fully dressed, and she had been lying on a plank bed, her head pillowed on a rough cushion.

Where was she? What had happened? She asked herself these questions in trembling agitation.

And then in a flood memory came back; and she struggled to her feet with a sharp little cry.

That night . . . when her husband had died, and she had tried to escape with Derek Capel.

Then the police had come, and—

An agonised cry came from her stiff lips, and she looked wildly around her. Where was she?

Her eyes made out a small, cell-like apartment, with a stout door, at the top of which was a grating. The electric light from a corridor filtered through, casting thin shafts of light. More by instinct than anything else the gently nurtured wife of Professor Appleby guessed the truth.

She was in a prison cell!

As the full realisation of this broke upon her, Eleanor with a little gasp rushed to the door and hammered upon it with her clenched hands. Short, gasping cries came from her lips; for the awful fear of four closed walls was upon her. She felt that she must get out or die.

Frenziedly she beat with her hands against the door. A sickening horror seized and almost paralysed her, blanching her face and turning her whole palpitant form icy cold. She was like a child that is lost and finds itself in the dark, and indeed, in that moment of her anguish and sorrow Eleanor looked more than ever like a beautiful child-woman. Presently a wardress came along.

'Oh, let me out! Let me out!' she cried with streaming eyes. The wardress tried to comfort her, for she was no hard woman—indeed, she was exceedingly kind-hearted—and she was moved to pity and compassion by Eleanor's captivating beauty, her youth and evident gentle breeding which had never known the degradation of prison cell.

'Why am I here? I have done nothing. I am innocent!' cried Eleanor again and again.

The wardress sighed. She was a buxom, ruddy-cheeked woman from Devonshire, and luckily for her her duties were mainly to comfort those in despair, for she could not be stern. She knew the facts of this case, and a sordid enough affair it seemed to be, yet she could not believe that a girl so young and innocent could be guilty of such a crime.

She did her best to soothe Eleanor and to explain.

'It is only for a time, my dear. Oh, my poor lamb! Why did you try to escape the police? Then this would never have come to you. But it is only for a time. The coroner's inquest is tomorrow, or the day after, and then you will be proved to be innocent and go free. Come, don't fret yourself. Now let me get you a little of something nice to eat.'

But her words, meant to soothe, only caused the wildest alarm to Chief Inspector Brent's latest captive. It drove the realisation of her awful plight home to her. The world rocked and reeled for Eleanor Appleby. The wardress's concern changed to alarm as she watched her, for she saw the blood ebb from cheeks and lips; noted the ashy pallor that succeeded and the strange motion of her hands. Eleanor staggered, fell against the door of her cell, and as the wardress groped frantically for her keys, the girl slid to the stone floor of her cell in a dead swoon.

The wardress was quick to open the door, fearing that this second swoon, so soon after the first, might be serious, and she was about to lift the unconscious girl when along the corridor strode Doctor Alec Portal, followed by Chief Inspector Brent, very grim and creased of visage.

These two were at daggers drawn. Doctor Portal was savagely angry and most amazingly full of fight. He had managed to instil a little sullen awe even into constitutional authority as represented by New Scotland Yard and Chief Inspector Brent in particular.

He turned on the famous criminologist, his fair face hawklike as he saw Eleanor's unconscious form lifted on to the plank in the cell.

'It is as I expected,' he said, his voice throbbing and savage. 'She is very ill. Your barbarian conduct has produced a very critical condition, inspector, and I warn you that if any serious results attend it I shall lay the blame at your door. I warned you that I was her doctor, and that she was in a state of nervous exhaustion. It was your duty to take medical advice before pursuing such a course as this.'

'Tssh, man!' snapped the inspector fiercely; 'I know my duty. Plans had been made for her to escape from the country, and my duty was to stop that.'

Doctor Portal, refusing to quibble any longer, turned to his patient. A strange, shivering thrill shot along his nerves, and his heart beat furiously at sight of her again. He who had for so long dedicated his life to his work, with never a thought of women, had now come face to face with a fundamental fact.

How cold she was—how cold! And yet how beautiful! Why, she was little more than a lovely child! And yet fashioned exquisitely in the mould of a woman. As she lay there half on her side, her fair hair lying in gleaming waves around her slim shoulders, her rather skimpy costume revealed to the full the glorious seductive curves of her figure.

But he pulled himself together and bent to his work with professional deftness and care. Doctor Alec Portal's keen, intellectual face became very grave as he administered restoratives, with no effect. The minutes passed, and even the inspector behind him began to fidget. So prolonged and deathlike was the swoon that Doctor Portal began to think, with a wild pounding of his heart, that she was beyond his medical attention and care.

This was no ordinary fainting fit!

His medical experience told him that her condition necessitated an extremely delicate and swiftly performed surgical operation. Only a slight one it is true, yet it needed nerves and skill to perform it. It was a task for a Harley Street specialist, and even so, the issue hung on the most delicate balance.

For a moment Alec Portal quailed at the thought that, however unwittingly, he might, by some error of judgment, pronounce sentence of eternal slumber on this frail and ethereal sleeping beauty.

Yet he was a man. And he was made to love a woman. The thing that had never touched him yet—passion at its finest and cleanest—had wakened to life in him. And now it bade him save his mate, to claim her for his own.

He took out his lancet, and rolled up one of Eleanor's sleeves, exposing the perfect moulding of the snowy arm.

'Just hold the arm, inspector, so as to keep it steady.'

The Yard man complied, and Doctor Alec Portal bent to his task, his brows knit in concentration and his blue eyes gleaming. Soon there was a little gush of blood staining the ivory of the girl's arm crimson. Doctor Alec Portal continually staunched the flow, and at length applied a tourniquet. To his satisfaction the heart commenced to beat more normally.

And soon Eleanor's inky lashes, like black butterflies on her pallid cheeks, fluttered upwards, and her brown eyes looked wonderingly, uncomprehendingly into Doctor Alec Portal's. All at once it seemed memory came to her, and a look of childish fear flashed like summer lightning into her eyes.

She tried to start up.

'Oh, please—please— You are my friend!' she cried pitifully.

'Take me away from here. They are saying that I did it, that I killed him! But I didn't. I swear it!'

'Yes, yes—hush, child!' the doctor cried soothingly. 'Come, drink this.' He tried to force a silver flask of brandy to her lips, but with a gesture of repugnance she refused it.

'A little water, please,' she said faintly. Her brown eyes dilated; she looked around her huntedly. 'Oh—I shall die if they keep me here,' she gasped.

The wardress gave her water, and she closed her eyes and fell back.

Doctor Portal, with a significant look at Inspector Brent, withdrew for a minute.

'Now, inspector,' he said aggressively, 'I demand the instant release of this unfortunate and innocent lady. You may have taken out a warrant for arrest, but I imagine you will not care to execute it before the coroner's inquest, and without doing so you cannot detain her any longer.'

Inspector Brent's eyes glinted under his shaggy brows. He was convinced of Eleanor Appleby's guilt.

'I may detain anyone in England on suspicion for twenty-four hours without entering a charge,' he said doggedly. 'I am within my rights, and I shall have her remanded on suspicion—'

'Tush, man; do you want to kill her?' Doctor Portal exclaimed savagely. 'I will act as security for her safe keeping. She must have nursing and care, and I am going to take her to my mother's home.'

Eventually the taciturn inspector concurred in this arrangement, and Eleanor was half-carried out and helped into the doctor's big saloon car. With his face somewhat relaxed Alec Portal whirled his precious charge away to his mother's home.

All the same there was a vague stirring of dread in the doctor's heart.

He did not like the queer mingling of combativeness and triumph in Inspector Brent's attitude towards him. It was as though he knew something, and was sure of his victim. Eleanor,

too, resting against the cushions at the back of the car, looked
like a haunted creature. He was afraid for her. He wished the
next few days well over.

Alec's mother, a beautiful, silver-haired old lady, received
Eleanor with every kindness, and the next three days were days
of almost untrammelled rest and delicious peace for the girl.
Doctor Portal ordered her to remain in bed, and she was inun-
dated with flowers and fruit and gifts of all sort; friends she
had known before her marriage, and whom the professor had
debarred from his house, came to see her, and they were all
very gentle and kind, so much so that Eleanor began to wonder.

She began to notice curious looks that they cast at one
another when they were together at her bedside. Eleanor's mind
by now was in a curiously dreamy state. She could not make
it all out. Sometimes the memory of her husband would come
. . . and that night of horror. It would come like a blinding pain
in her head.

If she mentioned her husband those around her would say
'Hush, dear—all that is past!'

And Eleanor was only too willing to forget. Only too willing!
It all seemed like a bad dream—that night, and the dreadful
hours that had followed the discovery of Professor Appleby
dead in his chair.

Doctor Portal watched her with a certain amount of uneasiness. He was not quite sure that his treatment was as
satisfactory as it seemed. The transformation was so sudden
and complete. Eleanor seemed so completely happy; a little
quiet, perhaps, and dreamy. She adored Alec's mother, and
followed her wherever she went with her eyes. The girl's half-
parted lips, the tiny tinge of colour in her cheeks, and the soft
glow of serenity in her brown eyes told of an unnatural artificial
state to Doctor Alec Portal.

Her highly-strung nature, unable to bear the weight of
tragedy and anguish that had fallen upon her, had given way.
And sitting there in bed, with the white pillows propping her

up, her fair hair plaited round her shapely head, she just looked a very beautiful and adorable child.

Alec hated to undeceive her, to take the bandage from her eyes and reveal the sword of Damocles that hung above her head. But it had to be done. For on the third day the coroner's inquest was appointed to take place.

Alec's mother tried to soften the blow. Very, very timidly she came to the girl, all in black herself, and carrying soft, filmy black things in her hands. She sank down by the bedside. 'It's time for you to get up, my dear. We are going out this morning, in the car.'

Eleanor looked at the widow's weeds on the bed. Troubled, she looked at Alec's mother, who tried to smile at her, though her eyes were shining with blinding tears. 'But what are these?' Eleanor was going to ask—and then it came, that tearing, flashing pain in her head. And her brain came to a sharp focus.

'Oh!' she put her little hands to her head.

Alec's mother saw that the flood of memory was returning. Her heart cried out, for she recognised that the crisis was coming. She put in anxiously, gently: 'It is the inquest today. You will be brave. Oh, my dear; I know you are good and pure, and you have nothing to fear.'

Eleanor sat very white and still for a while with the horror back in her eyes. Her face was frozen. Then all at once the tears came to her relief, too, and she seized Mrs Portal's hand and kissed it again and again.

'You believe in me?' she cried pitifully. 'You do believe in me? Oh, I have a feeling that something dreadful is going to happen. But I will be brave,' she added, and she looked up suddenly with an odd expression in her eyes. 'I—I'm going to play the game through to the end.'

And so half an hour later they set out for the coroner's court, Eleanor and Doctor Portal side by side. The doctor was telling himself that the three days' surcease from sorrow and anguish had saved her reason. But he feared for what might yet happen.

Looking at the lovely face beside him in the car, pure in its frozen calm as some marble lily, Alec Portal vowed to himself that she was innocent and that he would yet save her from the final awful result that, whether directly or otherwise, her husband's cruelty threatened to bring about.

'Hallo!' exclaimed Alec Portal sharply all at once.

He had turned the car into the street which led directly to the court, and now the car's progress was barred; for the whole street was a seething mass of human heads, straining to catch sight of the lovely young wife who was said to have poisoned her brilliant professor husband.

For the first time during the drive Eleanor showed acute emotion. She wrung her hands, and crouched back, her face wreathed in anguish. The eyes of the curious sightseers seemed to bore into her. A few gave pitying exclamations at sight of her plight and turned away, but their places were quickly taken by the throng that pressed ever on.

Doctor Portal and Eleanor were saved by two mounted police who cleared the street and made an avenue through the press for the car to reach the court. Even so they were forced to run the gauntlet of the crowd's gaze, and listen to its varied remarks, an experience which seared Eleanor's mind indelibly with horror.

But that was only the first confused impression in what seemed a never closing phantasmagoria of terror and dread. Next she was in the coroner's court, a small, dusty apartment of long benches from which a sea of faces stared at Eleanor.

She remembered seeing Derek Capel. It seemed he would never take his eyes off her. Though she had but a vague impression of him, he appeared more dissolute, more reckless than ever. His eyes were haunting her, begging, pleading and threatening alternately. It appeared he wanted to say something to her. But some inward voice prompted her to take as little notice of him as possible.

And Vera! She was there, flaunting herself in one of her mistresses' hats. Superb confidence and insolence played in her smile. Malice steeled to do its worst shone in her eyes. She looked about the court as though she were quite familiar with such surroundings and rather enjoyed being there.

There fell a death-like hush in the crowded room as the coroner entered by a side door and took his seat. He appeared a stern, formidable figure; his face, with its high forehead, rather hooked nose and thin, compressed lips seemed as if carved in wax in the white glare of light that fell upon him. He gazed around the court with keen, penetrating eyes, and at last they rested on Eleanor, and it seemed to the girl that they were filled with a dread accusation.

The jury were empanelled. And then to Eleanor there followed a confused blur of events. The court was filled with a monotonous hum. People utterly unknown to her stepped into the witness-box and gave evidence. She knew that she should be following the proceedings with close attention, but she was unable to do so. Her heart was filled with a numbling loneliness and despair. She felt indescribably old and tired, and all she knew was that she wanted to creep away somewhere and be alone.

Someone had moved quietly to her side. It was Alec Portal, and he was speaking in low tones that held an undercurrent of strained excitement.

'This is he—Doctor Lasglow, the Home Office analyst. He was responsible for the post-mortem examination. And now we shall know the truth, and this deplorable business will be all over.'

A tall, spare man, almost bald, and with a keen, intellectual face was in the box. He took the oath quietly and gravely, and then the coroner was seen to lean forward in his seat.

'You have made an examination of the body and the organs of Professor Aldous Appleby: what is your considered opinion of the manner in which he met his death.'

'He died by poison,' was the answer, quietly and gravely given.

There was a great stir in court.

Doctor Alec Portal looked at Eleanor, and his eyes were filled with amaze and dread. She covered her face with her gloved hands and broke into a fit of violent shuddering.

Other questions followed, and the amazing information was elicited that the great Home Office expert, skilled though he was, was unable to designate the exact nature of the poison that had killed Professor Appleby. The organs of the stomach all indicated acute poisoning, but no traces of any known poison had been discovered.

The atmosphere in the court had by now become electric. All were craned forward to listen to the Home Office chemist. Newspaper reporters were scribbling hastily. This promised to become the most sensational and mysterious poisoning case of the century. And in his seat in the well of the court, Derek Capel leant forward, his face ghastly, his whole attention strained upon the chemist who was making these fateful disclosures.

'Yes; we have examined the whole of the contents of the medicine cabinet,' the expert declared quietly. 'We found many known poisons, but scarcely one which it is possible could have caused the death of the professor. Otherwise we should have found traces in the body. In "exhibit 19"'—the coroner was holding up the fateful little blue-black bottle marked 'Poison' which had so early arrested the attention of Inspector Brent—'we found strychnine in the form of hydrocholoride. Yes, sir, that is the bottle.'

'Is it possible,' the coroner asked, 'that Professor Appleby could have been poisoned by hydrochloride?'

'It is not, sir,' the expert answered emphatically. 'Otherwise we should have found traces in the body.'

Derek Capel leant back in his seat.

The case was rapidly assuming a bewildering aspect. And drama now followed swiftly. Another Government witness was called, a finger-print expert from Scotland Yard. He identified the little blue-black bottle, and spoke to having found finger marks.

'Are those finger marks identical with any finger-prints at present in possession of the authorities?' asked the coroner amidst tense and strained attention

'Yes, sir,' answered the detective. 'During, her period of detention we took the finger-prints of Mrs Eleanor Appleby, the deceased's wife. The finger-prints on the bottle are identical with those of Mrs Appleby.'

It was as if a thunderclap had burst in the court.

There was a loud and prolonged stir—an excited buzz of comment. The ushers sternly demanded silence. But little notice was taken for a time. All heads were craned to stare at her who was now the central figure in this amazing tragedy.

Eleanor had started upright. Her eyes were transfixed by the little blue-black bottle which the coroner had now placed again on the desk. A deadly faintness seized her, and it was noticeable that her whole slim figure in the flowing widow's weeds which so tragically became her was trembling violently. A long moment her burning eyes were fixed on 'exhibit 19,' and with half-parted lips she strove to speak. At last the words came in a tragic cry.

'That bottle! I saw it on the night. Oh, mother—help your girl! What could I have been thinking of—what could I have been thinking of?'

She relapsed into her seat, her whole slim body shaken by dry, hard sobs. Otherwise there was a dead silence in the court.

Alec put his arm around her, and fought against a cold douche that seemed to flood all his sympathy. No, no—not that! It couldn't be that she . . . What was she saying? Poor child! In her overwrought state she was near to delivering herself into the hands of the Philistines.

He tried to comfort her.

'Hush, hush! Don't cry so. Don't let these lawyers and people confuse you.'

He managed to soothe her a little, half-leaning against him, her whole body palpitant, her lashes trembling against her smooth, pale cheeks. Doctor Alec Portal inwardly anathematised the court—the whole business. They had brought her to a dangerously overwrought state.

The coroner was meticulously arranging papers on his desk.

He looked over at the jury box. 'You are to remember,' he said in his most precise tones, 'that the bottle, "exhibit 19", contained hydrocholoride which it is impossible could have caused the death of Professor Appleby. The point is very important.'

But it is doubtful whether it impressed the jury. They had just seen sheer startled fear and guilt on a woman's face, and they had been shocked by the vivid impression of it.

Then followed another witness, Vera, the house parlourmaid. Her vulgar nature delighted in the white glare of publicity. She was breathing in the rarefied atmosphere of fame, or notoriety. She gave her evidence with gusto, indeed, with something of the verve and effect of a dramatic actress.

'. . . And I came rushing into the study to find the professor in his death throes in the chair,' she told a hushed court. 'She was there, pale as a sheet'—referring to Eleanor—'holding on to the curtain, she was, and watching him like a cat.

'He looked all round as the others came in, and there was froth on his lips. Ghastly he looked, and his throat was rattling. He was trying to speak. At last he got it out. "Someone's poisoned me," he said, and he pointed—at her!'

At this point the coroner sternly admonished the witness, asking her to give her evidence with a little more decorum and fewer gestures. His rebuke served to heighten the almost hysterical atmosphere in the court.

'And then what happened?' the coroner asked sharply. 'Tell us in as few words as possible.'

'He asked for a drink—Mr Capel, that is. He said he wanted to pull himself together. That seemed to wake the mistress up as if out of a dream. She took up the port decanter, and then with a little scream she let it drop, and it broke into a thousand pieces on the floor.'

'Hardly a thousand pieces,' the coroner said dryly. 'You exaggerate.'

A solicitor on the side of what was virtually the prosecution jumped up. 'I have a witness who will put it in as evidence that the decanter was found smashed in several large parts,' he said. 'It was of English cut glass, and the stem, or neck, bore a finger-print which is identical with one of those taken of Mrs Appleby's.'

Again there was a hubbub in the court. When a stern repri-mand from the coroner had at length quelled the excited disturbance, Eleanor Appleby's name was called as a witness.

She appeared quite dazed as she rose to her feet, and a warder helped her into the witness-box. Alec Portal's heart bled for her as he watched the slight, girlish form in black walking with faltering steps across the intervening space. And a murmur of sympathy and admiration rose from the crowded court as they saw the delicate, exquisite face of this child-woman who was suspected of murdering her husband by administering poison.

Her mass of lovely hair was almost hidden by the widow's veil she wore, but fair tendrils of it curled about her temples; her creamy-white skin appeared like marble by reason of the shock she was sustaining, and which was palpable in her large brown eyes that appeared too big for her little oval face.

The coroner looked at her and sighed. Could guilt really be masked by this fair semblance of youth and innocence.

He leant towards her. 'Just answer the questions put to you,' he said gently. 'You are distraught. Remember that the law takes no heed of this, however, and do not in confusion run any risk of contradicting your own statements.'

She tried to stay the fluttering of her white hands on the rail. She drew herself up proudly, and her sweet eyes met his frankly and candidly. As she spoke her voice thrilled through the court, clear and pure.

'Thank you. I appreciate the motive of your warning, but I have nothing to conceal.'

Involuntarily his manhood did homage to her grace and dignity, and he bowed his head gravely.

It was poor Eleanor's last desperate stand, however. When the questions came with machine-gun rapidity she became terribly confused, the colour flamed and went in her cheeks, and her voice, when she answered, was low and indistinct.

It became painful to wait for her answers.

'You were asleep? ... Yes?—oh, no, you say. You were aroused by the breaking of the vase. Were you the first to arrive in the study? Your bedroom was situated exactly overhead the study. Did you hear any sounds of a struggle?'

And so on, *ad infinitum*. The witness constantly contradicted herself. Her lips moved, and would utter no words. The jury listened and watched her compassionately, but they were to do their duty, and they had already decided that they could return but one verdict.

'Your husband was cruel to you, was he not? ... What form did his cruelty take? ... Oh, you cannot say. Did he threaten you with cruelty on this particular night? Yes? What did he threaten? Please try to speak up.'

She shook her head helplessly.

Derek Capel watched it all, his handsome, rather dark face working convulsively. Several times he almost started up with hands clenching and unclenching, but something chained him to his seat. Horror—fear—all the emotions of which mankind is capable, fleeted across his face. Tears of anguish appeared in his eyes, and he was like a soul in torment. He loved this woman—loved her madly. And before his eyes she was going through Hell.

Doctor Alec Portal was almost in the same condition of mind, except that he had more faith, more self-control. He believed in her. He believed her innocent as an angel above. Nothing could shake him, and he told himself that if there was a law to punish the wicked and uphold the just—if the law were not a wicked and outrageous mockery—then in a very short time this painful inquisition would be over, and she would be free.

Alec Portal sat with white teeth clenched in his tanned face, his blue eyes gleaming straight into her dear face. It was as though he were trying to give her some of his own superb self-control, the steel nerves that had stood him in such good stead in the operating theatre.

'Speak up, little thing—oh, my dear, look up and tell him it is a lie.'

For the coroner was speaking, and from his lips with terrific intentness came the words: 'Now, please tell us, did you or did you not take up the wine decanter? And did it drop from your hands, or did it crash to the floor from the table as you brushed past it?'

Eleanor looked up piteously, the tears streaming from her eyes.

'I—I, oh, don't ask me!' she cried, her voice ringing once more clear and sweet as a bell throughout the court. 'Heaven help me, whatever I did that night, I swear I meant him no harm. I don't remember, I—I didn't mean to do it. Oh, please have mercy!'

She stopped. She could not go on, though it was evident that she was trying to say something more. In the eyes of more than one of the jurors the tears of emotion glistened.

Alec Portal was standing up. He was not conscious of what he was doing, but across the empty space that divided him from Eleanor, he sent her all that he had in him—his will-power pent up, and screwed down to terrific compressions—bidding her take a hold on herself, that just for this moment her dear life itself was at stake.

Her lips parted—moving; she was trying to speak as she swayed in the dock.

'I—I— Yes, it is true,' she said, very quietly and simply, with her eyes closed like one in a mesmeric trance, 'I dropped the decanter!'

There was a shout in the court, a mad, husky shout: 'Eleanor!'—It came from Derek Capel, wild-eyed, haggard.

But Eleanor did not look at him. She swayed where she stood, like a slender reed in the wind, and then quietly and with only a sighing breath, she slid to the floor of the witness-box.

Whilst they were carrying her away the coroner ordered those parts of the court admitting the general public to be cleared.

The hearing of the case lasted only a little time longer. The evidence of Inspector Brent was taken, and that of other police experts. The police said very little. It was evident they were satisfied so far with their case, and at length the jury retired.

They were absent half an hour, during which early editions of the London evening newspapers came damp from the press, and were sold like hot cakes. A vast throng was being moved on by the police outside the coroner's court. The interest of the general public in what had now become known as 'The Poisoned Professor Case' had reached fever heat.

In the court, Doctor Alec Portal sat with his head in his hands, waiting, hoping against hope. His faith in Eleanor was not shaken. He realised that she had given damning evidence against herself, but he knew—none better than he!—that she was not responsible for what she was saying.

All around him he heard people discussing the case in low, whispered tones. He saw an eminent K.C. shake his head sorrowfully: 'Poor woman! She must have had a hell of a time with that man! Oh, you can't get away from it—she put the poison in the decanter. They'll find traces of it in the body yet!'

'A damned shame!' said someone else. 'She'll get off with manslaughter, though. A dashed pretty woman, too, by gad!'

The young doctor felt that he could bear it no longer. Manslaughter! Eleanor—manslaughter! That meant imprisonment for life. But she was innocent—innocent, pure and good! He could have staked his life on it.

The ringing of a bell! That meant that the jury were returning. The court was miraculously crowded again, and amidst a deathly silence the coroner entered by the side door, and took his place in the high oaken seat.

The jurymen filed in gravely. They looked very white and shaken, and the foreman upset a glass of water as he rose to the question: 'Gentlemen of the jury, have you considered your verdict?'

'Are you agreed?'

'Yes.'

'We find,' said the foreman of the jury in a voice that was not quite steady, 'that Professor Appleby died from poison administered by his wife, Eleanor Appleby.'

Doctor Alec Portal heard it, and got up and walked from the court. He could not look at the woman he loved. He knew that she was in the court, pale as alabaster, but trembling no longer. He had seen her, looking like one who is in a beautiful trance, and as he walked headlong down the street he cursed the dead, cursed the fiend whose hatred and cruelty had pursued her beyond the grave.

'He was insane,' Doctor Alec Portal whispered to himself. 'He killed himself, cunningly—cleverly, so that she might suffer. Oh, I know it! That is the solution of the mystery.'

And in the court a police officer was gently detaining Eleanor whilst it was being cleared of the general public. At length Chief Inspector Brent descended to where she sat, and his grizzled face was compassionate. He had been chiefly instrumental in pursuing her and trapping her in the mesh of the law, but he had come almost to hate the duty he had set himself to perform.

'Madam,' he said quietly and gravely, looking down at some papers he held in his hand. 'You know me. I am Chief Inspector Brent of Scotland Yard, and I have a warrant—'

'I know—I know,' she gulped, looking up. 'I quite understand. Please do not go on. Oh, God!' she cried in her agony, 'help me to bear up under this awful outrage perpetrated under the name of law!'

But the law is not to be denied. Chief Inspector Brent's droning voice went on, as he read from his papers:

'WHEREAS at an inquest held at X—, T— county on the twenty-seventh day of October before Jeremiah Johns, Esq., Coroner of said county, on the body of Aldous Luke Appleby, there lying dead, by the jurors whose names are hereto subscribed . . .

'The said jurors upon their oath do say that Aldous Luke Appleby came to his death on the night of Thursday, October twenty-sixth, by poison taken internally. And from all the evidence brought before them the jury believe that the poison was administered by the hand of his wife, Eleanor Appleby.

'In testimony whereof the said jurors have hereunto set their hands this . . .'

Inspector Brent stopped, peering over his papers. For the second time within an hour Eleanor Appleby had swooned.

CHAPTER V

THE final battle was raging around Eleanor Appleby. Long ago the Grand Jury had returned a true bill against her, and she had been committed for trial. Four months of dread and agony of suspense had unnerved her, changed her completely, yet only to make her more ethereally beautiful than ever, more childlike in her innocent guilelessness. No longer was she even a woman fighting for her life and honour. She seemed utterly unable to realise the dreadful issues at stake. And as she stood in the dock, facing the judge in his wig and gown, sometimes looking round wonderingly at the sea of faces in the well of the court, or facing the battery of scrutinising eyes turned on her from the jury-box, her air was wistfully eager—childishly pathetic— as one who thinks she has done some wrong, and is sorry for the pain and trouble caused by it to others.

It was an attitude that, all unwittingly on her part, blunted the terrible weapons that the prosecution had ready to use against her.

The case had been put down for hearing at the Central Criminal Courts at Old Bailey, and Lord Justice Horlinge, one of the most humane and keenly penetrative of the High Court judges the bar had ever known, was hearing it. It had foregathered before the bench a dazzling array of forensic talent and legal ability. Sir Hugo Rattenbury, the eminent K.C. and criminal lawyer, was leading for the Public Prosecutor, and the brief for the defence had been entrusted to the fashionable David Greatorex, whose meteoric progress across the legal firmament was being guided by his wonderful voice, his merciless, uncanny faculty for cross-examination, and his biting wit that so swiftly brought ridicule upon a hostile witness.

He was supported by a host of minor legal lights, and into

the defence of Eleanor Appleby he had thrown all his charac-
teristic force and energy, allied to a passionate fervour that
bespoke his own deep-rooted belief in her innocence.

The case for the prosecution had been clearly and abundantly
stated. Chief Inspector Brent had given his evidence, and he
had seemed in very heavy humour about it—entirely unlike the
brisk, soldierly police officer whose reputation in the conduct
of such cases was so high. He studiously avoided looking at
the prisoner more than was absolutely necessary, whilst Eleanor,
for her part, watched him at first with half-parted lips, a wistful,
eager look on her face, which gradually changed to cold despair.

During the long wait for her trial Eleanor had been stricken
down with brain fever, and at one time she had been walking
perilously near to the Valley of the Shadow. During those awful
days of fever, when she had lain tossing in her bed in the
hospital, Chief Inspector Brent had visited her many times.

Indeed, it was he who had comforted her—not Doctor Alec
Portal—he who had told her at length that he believed in her
innocence, and had held her hand and assured her that from
the bar of Justice she would go forth a free woman, with honour
untarnished. The grizzled old veteran of the Yard had been
obviously moved by her innocence and childish beauty; he had
listened to her delirious ravings, and from them he could gain
nothing that would bolster up his case against her.

And so he had told her in the end that he was her friend.
And because she so pathetically wanted to believe—because it
is those who oppress us most we do believe in and respect—his
words had brought to Eleanor a blessed joy and relief. They
had brought the relief of tears to her—tears that undoubtedly
saved the racked and tortured woman's brain, and caused her
to mend both physically and mentally.

And so she had been brought to this. She had been saved
for the public sacrifice, Inspector Brent, with the conscious
shame of a Judas, poured out a damning indictment of her in
the box, and would not look at her. He was a man of simple,

straightforward honesty himself, but cursed with a dogged and obstinate nature. And thinking the whole matter over in his own quiet watches, he had decided that he must be right—that the professor had been poisoned, and that none other but his wife could have administered that poison to him. The law had been outraged, and must be vindicated

What travail it cost him to give his evidence no man guessed. He felt as if the brand of Cain was on his own forehead as he saw the prisoner, a delicate figure in black, shrink farther back in the dock, and as he finished she kept her face averted, shivering preceptibly.

But now David Greatorex, chief counsel for the defence, had risen, his dark, resolute, sternly-chiselled face, cold yet handsome as some faultless god, a singular smile curving his lips as he gazed at the witness in the box.

'You say that on the early morning of the tragedy, after the prisoner had again retired to her room, you and other officers made a thorough examination of the study in which Professor Appleby came by his death?'

Inspector Brent: 'That is so.'

'And amongst other things you discerned "Exhibit 19"—this little blue-black bottle marked "Poison". Now there was a full cabinet of various chemicals and various poisons in that study. Why did your attention particularly alight on this blue-black bottle?'

'Because—' The Inspector hesitated.

'Now, come, come! Answer me. Be careful what you say.'

'Because since I had arrived at the house, and during the time I was making my inquiries, I saw one of those in the room glancing repeatedly across at the medicine cabinet. And since she was fairly near the cabinet, I was satisfied in my own mind that she was looking at this black bottle.'

The great K.C. smiled—a bleak smile of scorn.

'I notice you use the feminine gender in speaking of this person. But Mrs Appleby, you say, was standing over at the mahogany table that held the wine and spirit decanters. Therefore, according to this plan of the study, she could not have been "fairly near the medicine cabinet". Who, then, was this person you saw glancing at the black bottle?'

Inspector Brent bit his lip slightly. 'It was Vera Cummings, the house parlourmaid, sir,' he answered challengingly.

'Ah!'

Counsel arranged some papers before him, whilst a tiny smile of scorn played about the corners of his mouth. 'This witness,' he said dryly, 'appeared to know a great deal of what went on at the Lodge, and particularly of the happenings of that night. I understand she is to be called next into the box, and it is possible that more information may be elicited from her.'

He sat down then, amidst a stir. It was palpable that he made a point with the jury, who turned the battery of their attention keenly on the next witness as she stepped into the box.

Vera, the late house parlourmaid at the Lodge, had imitated her mistress, in that she was garbed suitably in mourning. She retained her self-possession admirably, and took the oath in clear tones. She promised to be what the bar describes as 'a good witness,' except that there was just a hint of brazen defiance in her attitude—something that was faintly repellent to the court. Quite boldly and openly she looked across at the prisoner in the dock, and smiled. It was an impudent smile of sheer unmitigated malice.

For the first time Eleanor roused herself to the proceedings. The statue throbbed into life, drew herself up proudly; and with a haughty poise of her head, her grand eloquent brown eyes looked up at the witness, and bore the challenge.

For fully a moment eye met eye, soul looked into soul, with only a few feet of space dividing prisoner from witness. And it was Vera's eyes that dropped first, her face that flamed scarlet and then withered to an ashen pallor. She fidgeted on her feet.

But as she told her story her voice warmed and became scornful; the tiny licking flame of malice crept again into her eyes as she repeatedly glanced across at her former mistress.

'They was always quarrelling,' she told a rapt court. 'Night after night I'd hear high words between them.'

Counsel for the prosecution rose. 'And what was the attitude of the accused during these nightly quarrels? You say that the professor appeared to have much to grumble at. He accused her of having no knowledge of household economy, told her that she was a worthless wife. Did not the accused make some reply to these charges?'

'Oh, she never said anything,' Vera exclaimed contemptuously. 'She just looked at him with those eyes of hers. I think that made it worse. Dumb insolence, he used to call it.'

'Indeed,' counsel said dryly. 'Did she never make any sound?'

'Sometimes she used to scream,' Vera supplied dramatically.

David Greatorex rose at once. 'I am glad the witness has said that,' he put in, with the scornful smile quirking at his lips. 'It is a point that I wish to emphasise. I shall show that the deceased used actual physical cruelty towards his wife, and that she bore, all this for two years with wonderful patience and endurance.'

Vera continued her story of what had happened that night. With considerable dramatic force she told now the smashing of the vase had awakened her from sleep; how the cries and groans of the dying man had brought her hastening to the study, to find her mistress in dressing-gown and slippers, standing by the table that bore the decanters, and staring with affrighted eyes at her husband.

Then came the damning conclusion, the story of how Eleanor had dropped the decanter, smashing it on the bare boards round the fringe of the carpet.

It was obvious that her dramatically told story could not fail to have its profound effect upon the jury. Vera preened herself in conscious triumph. She was in the limelight once more—the limelight that she loved. The hushed and strained attention of the court had been given to her in full. But now David Greatorex was rising to cross-examine her.

'You say that you were awakened by a thud—a crash as of something breaking?'

'Yes.'

'But only half an hour before you had admitted Mr Derek Capel as a visitor to the Lodge. Did you hear him go?'

Vera, rather hesitatantly: 'Yes, sir.'

'Oh, but then, according to witnesses' accounts, only ten minutes elapsed after the departure of Mr Capel before the crash was heard in the study. Do you say that time was longer or do you still say that you went to sleep and were awakened by the crash?'

'I went to sleep,' Vera persisted sullenly.

'And then you heard a crash and groans. And you came hastily into the study. You were the second to arrive, and you found Mrs Appleby clinging to the curtains and staring at her husband?'

'Yes,' said Vera in a low voice now. She sensed a trap.

'Other maidservants arrived after you. They also were in dressing-gowns and night attire. Am I correct in saying, however, that you were fully dressed, even to your maid's cap and apron?'

The woman bit her lips. She had been easily lured into it. The judge was looking up and across at her, as if waiting critically for her answer to this question. And Vera, the house parlourmaid, sought desperately for a shot in her locker with which to riposte to this dangerous cross-examiner.

'I went to sleep on the bed in my clothes,' she flamed at him. 'I had a feeling that something was going to happen that night.'

'Oh, indeed?'—gravely. 'We will leave that point for a moment, though it is of great interest. Now, since you were in your clothes you could have got down to the study as quickly as anyone else. Yet not quickly enough to see the vase break, I presume?'

His raised eyebrows as he asked this question stung her. 'What do you mean?' she asked passionately. 'Do you suggest that I was there? That I saw anything that happened beforehand?'

David Greatorex, K.C.: 'Rather the reverse. I suggest that you could not have known what had crashed in pieces and

roused you. I suggest that it might have been the decanter
tself falling from Professor Appleby's hands as he collapsed in
n apoplectic fit.'

'Rubbish,' Vera sneered, looking over at the jury. 'I saw her
with the decanter in her hands, and I saw her break it.'

'The inference you wish to convey to his Lordship and the
ury,' said David Greatorex smoothly, 'is that Mrs Appleby had
guilty knowledge of the contents of the port decanter, and that
he broke it, wishing to destroy what might prove to be strong
evidence for the prosecution?'

'Yes,' Vera said doggedly, and set her bag on the edge of the
witness-box with a little toss of her head.

'Then, can you suggest why the accused should wait until you
and others had arrived upon the scene before doing so?' asked
he great K.C. with a deprecating smile. 'If Mrs Appleby smashed
he decanter of deliberate intent—and it is strongly denied that
he did so—she would surely not wait to do it before two maids.'

There was a titter in the court at this. Vera, with eyes stabbing
pite, flung up her head.

'She didn't think of it before,' she averred dogmatically.

'Unlike you she did not appear to think of everything,'
counsel for the defence said gently. 'You even thought there
might possibly be a tragedy that night, so you went to bed in
our clothes. It suggests uncanny foresight to me. Let us
examine this remarkable omniscience of yours more closely.
You appeared to know everything that went on between your
master and your mistress.'

'It is a wicked innuendo,' the maid said hotly. 'It is not true.'

Opposing counsel had primed her to make this reply to any
charge of eavesdropping or spying. But David Greatorex only
shook his head slightly, as a duck might shake off water. 'You
were interested,' he insisted. 'Come now, admit that you were
intensely interested in everything that went on between them.'

'I deny it,' the maid answered loudly. 'It is a lie.'

'You have told the court that they slept in separate bedrooms, that they never cohabited as far as you knew. You have shown us that Professor Appleby exercised a subtle and malignant cruelty towards his wife. Yet you deny all interest in these proceedings. Has Mrs Appleby ever been unkind to you?'

'No.'

'But you will not deny that you were and have been antagonistic towards her?'

The woman's voice throbbed out passionately: 'I can't help what I say. I'm here on oath to speak the truth. I'm only one of those that's brought in to give evidence and help justice to be done.'

'A very good answer too,' said the noted K.C. dryly. 'Let us have some more of the truth then. Can you explain your feeling that something was going to happen on the night of the twenty-sixth?'

'I just had the feeling,' she answered. 'It was intuition. I was all keyed up with a sort of feverish excitement.'

'Indeed! Nothing else conduced towards that feeling? You cannot tell us whether you had any little disturbing adventure of your own during the evening?'

His keen eyes seemed to pierce her, and she paled with agitation all at once.

'What do you mean?' she almost gasped.

'I want the truth about your interest in the Applebys,' he rapped out sternly. 'You say you had no peculiar interest in them. You have no antagonism towards the accused, but wish merely to see justice done. Do you still say that, when I put it to you that for half an hour on the night of the twenty-sixth—and only two hours preceding the tragedy—you were alone with Professor Appleby in his study?'

She reeled backwards, as if struck a sudden violent blow, and in such deadly manner had counsel delivered it that it was obvious the witness was badly 'floored.'

All the court saw her demeanour, and a buzz of horrified amaze ran through its ranks. This woman had been alone with the professor on the night of his death. This was a fact of the most vital significance that she had not divulged, otherwise it would have been in the depositions. The thought inevitably occurred to every man in the jury box that if the professor had been poisoned here was one person at least who had had an opportunity to do it. And she might also have had a motive. Vera, the house parlourmaid, was what the newspapers delight to call in such cases 'a mystery woman.'

David Greatorex rolled his brief in his white tapering hands. His eyes were sparkling with a cold, merciless light, and his voice was keen, incisive, sounding audibly in every part of the court

'Come, now, will you please tell the court whether what I suggested is true?'

The witness made a desperate effort to rally. 'It is not true!' she said hoarsely. 'Not true.'

There was a significant pause. Counsel for the defence turned with that ruthless, derisive smile of his to the witness-box. Vera was staring in front of her as if she saw her own grave being dug.

'Not true?' repeated David Greatorex in gentle surprise as he turned again to her. 'Will you persist in that when I tell you that the accused will go into the witness-box, and part of her statement will be that she saw you alone with Professor Appleby in the study that night?'

'She lies!' Vera cried wildly and desperately. 'She's lying for some purpose of her own. It's all a tissue of lies.'

'I put it to the court that the witness who has just said that lies herself most foully,' cried counsel for the defence very sternly. 'I propose to examine her more particularly on this matter.

You had no association with Professor Appleby beyond that of master and servant?'

'No! No! Never!' Vera cried, entirely unnerved now.

'I suggest that you were his mistress,' counsel declared with sudden deadly intentness; 'that he had grown tired of you, and cast you off, and that for half an hour or more on the night of the twenty-sixth you were arguing with the deceased, pleading with him to do something for you.'

'It is all untrue,' she said hoarsely, like one dazed and sick. 'I never—he didn't—' She broke off to point a finger dramatically and passionately at Eleanor in the dock: 'This is what she has said about me!' she declared violently. 'It is a pack of dreadful lies!'

Eleanor, all in black, and almost calm, looked straight at the virago. And never had the accused woman looked quite so beautiful as in that moment. Her brown eyes, so large and compassionate, were fixed earnestly on the other, and in them glistened the tear-drops of utter pity. Her lips were tremulous. She was shedding real tears for this woman who had fallen, and whose soul was now being laid bare in the witness-box.

So the two women looked at one another, and then the maid herself at last burst into stormy tears. But if anything, she hated Eleanor Appleby more than ever at that moment.

David Greatorex, allowing a moment or two for this tableau to register itself on the minds of the court, resumed his attack. He was the consummate master of cross-examination. Every question probed like a keen and merciless scalpel now. She was a trapped creature in the box, and the whole court knew it.

'Come, let us have the truth of which you make such a proud boast. You admit you were his mistress?'

She roused, to turn on him like a tigress. 'It's a cruel and wicked lie!' she declared fiercely. 'Only she says that. *She* says she saw me in the study'—scornfully. 'No one else. No one can prove it.'

'Oh, indeed?' Counsel for the defence took up a piece of paper and unfolded it. 'I have here,' he said very slowly, 'a note in the deceased's handwriting. It was discovered in a certain part of the house, and was obviously addressed to you. For it commences "My darling Vera". I wonder whether you would care for me to read the rest aloud to the court,' he added, looking up.

Her breath came in strangled gasps. The famous K.C. turned where he stood and caused the note to be handed up to the judge by an usher. His lordship read it, and in a low voice declared that it must be read aloud, and then handed it to the jury. Witnesses must be called to substantiate the statement that it was in the deceased's handwriting.

'Thank you, my lord,' said counsel with a bow, and proceeded to read the letter to a stupefied court.

'My darling Vera,—I will come to you tonight. Do not be frightened, little one. She will never know. And, besides, what does it matter?'

'Will you now say that you were not the mistress of the deceased?' asked David Greatorex quietly. 'Do you still affirm that you had no interest—beyond that of a servant towards her employers—in the Applebys? In Professor Appleby in particular? Do you still swear that you did not spy on your mistress, that you did not hate her for being the rightful husband of the accused?'

Only wild sobs answered him from the box.

The remorseless voice went on: 'You were in the study that night with Professor Appleby? Come, now, were you, or were you not?'

'If she says so,' answered the woman, looking at him like a ghost.

'We may take it that the answer is in the affirmative,' said counsel suavely. He paused a moment to allow her sobs to abate. No one, however stern or strongly committed to the ideals of justice, could fail to feel a passing compassion for Vera Cummings then. She was a woman found out, deeply shamed and humiliated. She stood there as a liar and a perjurer, a woman of illicit loves—but now, suddenly, by the ruthless art of David Greatorex, K.C., she was to be cast into the rôle of suspect.

'Inspector Brent has told us that his attention was directed to the poison cabinet by your own glances, and in particular to "exhibit 19", the little blue-black bottle marked poison. Now, did anything transpire between you and the professor in connection with that bottle while you were in the study?'

Vera Cummings lost her nerve completely. She clutched the edge of the box. 'No! No—not that!' she cried, and her voice rose to a scream. 'You're trying to trap me. The poison bottle! . . . Oh, my God!'

The court was glad that her screaming voice stopped. It was a sound that tore at the nerves. She was sobbing again now, very near hysterics.

'You did not go to bed that night,' the voice went on. 'You did not go to sleep. You say yourself that you were expecting something to happen. What was it?'

The witness stopped sobbing all at once, as if arrested by some dread thought that had strayed out of the limbo of the forgotten past. White-faced, she stared unseeingly ahead of her, and her lips moved voicelessly. Then slowly she turned and looked queerly at counsel. Her lips moved again, and she repeated his own question in a voice little above a whisper.

'What was it? It came—and killed him! What was it?'

The spell was broken in the court as she threw up her hands with a shriek. Two wardresses carried her out of the witness-box in a state of collapse. There was a great rustling of papers in the court, and one or two women in the public gallery, unable to bear the nervous strain of listening to the trial any longer, made hastily for the exits.

David Greatorex was satisfied with his work. He turned and intimated to the judge that he had no further questions to ask the witness. Nor did the prosecution wish to examine her. They were dumbfounded, cast into consternation, and they wanted time to consider their position.

The case was adjourned until the following day. But it was thought it might conclude on the morrow, save perhaps, for counsel's concluding speeches and the judge's summing up. The trial had become a subject that was in everybody's mouth. Would Mrs Appleby get off? That was the burning question.

The public were not concerned with the question of her guilt or innocence. As usual, they were swayed by emotion. They were filled by pity and compassion for the tragic and beautiful figure in the box. She was a butterfly broken on the wheel. Married as a girl to a fiendishly cruel husband—why, she must have been through Hell! So the great British public argued. She had suffered enough. She deserved to get off. Poor woman!

Public feeling is curiously intangible, yet it travels far and carries enormous power and weight. It has crushed kings and lifted peasants to power, and those who are wise, who are publicists and statesmen, listen to its voice and obey its dictates.

The knowledgable ones amongst the public winked and said: 'Oh, yes; she did it all right. Wouldn't you? Fancy being tied to a mad genius! Take the business of the parlourmaid. Carrying on under the same roof. That was part of what she had to bear. But isn't Greatorex putting up a marvellous fight for her life? A brilliant lawyer, that chap!'

So the talk went round in public-houses and other places where people foregather. It so happened, not entirely by chance, that Dick Capel dropped into one such public-house on the evening of the first adjournment of the case. The public-house was in the vicinity of the Old Bailey, from which Derek could not tear himself away.

Capel Manor had not sheltered its owner for many a day. The whole place—the village itself!—seemed to fill him with dread. He must go where there was life, people—anything to distract his thoughts from Eleanor.

He loved her now more passionately than ever—worshipped her, indeed, as if she were a goddess. The mental torture and agony of suspense she was enduring were his to a far greater degree. There was scarcely a moment of his life that was not filled with bitter anguish. He was a man on the rack, tormented by his own thoughts.

And the experience through which he was passing had served to transfigure him. He was not the same old Derek Capel with glistening, dark hair, tanned face and the haunting, romantic eyes that went so well with his flashing smile. The change was subtle, yet vast. Lines had appeared in his face; he had become a little haggard, and in the depths of his eyes lurked fear.

Fear was a thing he had never known before. Daily he had hurtled through shrieking, shell-filled skies in a one-seater fighter 'plane during the war; recklessly, with a laugh on his lips. Pain of wounds—horrors—fear of death; nothing had ever made him quail until it came to the sight of a woman's marble-white, childish face with the great brown eyes bearing that piteous stricken look.

For the past five months the thought that Eleanor's health, her happiness, her life itself hung in the balance had had its effect, until, now that the crisis was near, he had become completely unnerved.

He entered the public-house, looking round him almost furtively, and gave a great start as he saw that the only other occupant, save the bartender, was a woman, smartly if vulgarly dressed. He could not fail to recognise her at once after staring at her for five hours during her ordeal in the witness-box. It was Vera, the late house parlourmaid at the Lodge.

Derek Capel hesitated a moment, and then walked to the bar and ordered draught champagne. He felt that he needed it, and with a somewhat shaky hand, that indicated this was not the first time his need had been met, he put it to his lips.

Vera was surveying him with dawning recognition in her bold eyes. She put down her glass of stout.

'Are you giving evidence tomorrow?' she asked with easy familiarity. She ignored their respective status as servant and employer, and perhaps the situation was unique.

His eyes were hostile as he leant on the bar.

'Why do you hate Mrs Appleby so?' he asked in a low, tense voice. 'She's done you no harm.'

'She took my man away,' the woman muttered sullenly. 'I wanted 'im—I 'ad need of 'im. She didn't want Professor Appleby; she hated him. But, well—you heard what they said in court. It was all the truth. And it was up to 'im to support me.'

'You fool!' he burst out in low, vibrant tones, seizing her wrist. 'He was insane. Things were crawling in his brain that night. I believe he would have killed her, or any other woman. You, perhaps. He was brooding mischief.'

A frightened gleam came into Vera's eyes. She began to sense something of what she had escaped. Professor Appleby had been too formidable for her that fateful night; she shuddered anew at the memory of his staggering anger when she had whispered her confidence to him.

Nevertheless, she snatched her hand away from Derek Capel's grasp with a show of sullen malice.

'Since you know so much,' she said acidly, 'why don't you tell the jury all you know? Why don't you tell 'em exactly what happened on that night?'

He stared at her with haunted eyes. 'What do you mean?' he rasped.

She laughed maliciously and leant towards him. 'Tell 'em all you know,' she said in a low voice, whilst she eyed him closely. 'Tell 'em what I saw that night, eh? . . . what you saw.' Her voice sank lower. 'Tell 'em the truth—that you saw Mrs Appleby actually put poison in the port decanter.'

She watched him closely to mark the effects of her words, but the cold horror seemed to have faded from his face as she proceeded, and now he threw back his head with a slightly forced laugh.

'Always the actress, eh, Vera?' he said harshly. 'Always lying. Trying to snare me now, eh? You know that neither you nor I saw any such thing. It might be more near the truth to say that you saw your own hand pouring the poison into the decanter. Good-night.'

And he left her biting her lips and staring ahead of her, her eyes glittering, and wondering what Derek Capel really did know.

CHAPTER VI

On the following morning a dense crowd invaded the Old Bailey, hoping for an opportunity to hear the proceedings during the resumption of the trial of Eleanor Appleby. It was in vain that the police tried to turn them away, and eventually formed them up into long queues; those who could not get into the court-room seemed content to wait outside for news.

They anticipated a speedy end to the trial. It seemed to be moving with all the certainty of a stage drama towards its conclusion. There was Derek Capel's evidence yet to come, and that was deemed important from many standpoints.

Calm and collected, if a trifle pale, Derek Capel stepped into the witness-box.

For a moment his eyes met Eleanor's. She smiled at him like a child, and something flared up in his eyes, the love and passion that shook him at times with galvanic force. But her eyes were cast down now, and the tiny flags of colour had mounted to her cheeks. Derek endeavoured to pull himself together.

He was soon being submitted to fire from heavy guns of interrogation and cross-examination brought up by the prosecution.

'You say you called at the Lodge at ten to twelve? Are you sure of the time?'

'. . . Oh, you are sure. Let us see whether you are sure of all the events that took place that evening. Now, what was your pretext for visiting the Lodge at so late an hour? A book. What was this book you say you lent to the deceased?'

'It was a valuable old edition on witchcraft, the art of herbalists, and concerning mediæval poisons,' answered Derek Capel steadily.

Counsel seized on this, and questions were hurled at the witness with machine-gun rapidity.

'Poisons? Do you know anything of poisons?' Derek Capel replied that he did not; he explained his possession of the book by telling the court that he collected old and rare editions. Sir Hugo Rattenbury peered at him through his gold-rimmed spectacles.

'Where is this book? Can you give the court that information?'

'I don't know,' Derek answered in a low voice.

Learned counsel looked scandalised. A rare volume, and he had mislaid it. Derek replied that he had left it with Professor Appleby. Was it there, demanded the cross-examining lawyer, when he returned to find the professor dead?

Derek replied that he could not recollect.

Counsel pounced on him, as a terrier does a rat, and tried to shake him with a bombardment of questions. Derek put up an imperturbable barrage. But the startling fact emerged that detectives had searched the house and had found no trace of the book. It was missing!

Here was another riddle to add to the many that this strange case presented.

Counsel for the prosecution came to the point whether Derek did or did not see Eleanor Appleby drop the port decanter.

'I did,' Derek said composedly in answer to the question. He did not look at the figure in the dock, but the nerves twitched visibly in his face.

Sir Hugo Rattenbury affected surprise.

'At another court you have said that Mrs Appleby did not drop the decanter. Do you now say that you were lying when you made that statement?'

'Yes, I was lying,' answered Derek Capel calmly. 'You see, I did not know which way the cat would jump. I meant to shield Mrs Appleby at whatever cost. But now I know positively that she dropped the decanter by accident. My suspicions were unworthy and base. You see,' he concluded with obvious triumph, 'no trace of poison has been discovered in the body.'

And that was the trump card of the defence. The Home Office pathologist was baffled, and he admitted it. Other experts spoke to tracing Mrs Appleby's finger-prints on the black bottle. But it contained a deadly poison whose effects were well known. Surely if it had been administered, traces would have been discovered in the body.

So the battle raged, until Eleanor Appleby, becoming confused and frightened, could detect but a blur of words, and stood as if in a trance, waiting for the end which seemed so long delayed.

A doctor—Professor Appleby's own doctor—went into the witness-box and swore that, as far as his knowledge went, the deceased had not been subject to epileptic fits. Then Doctor Alec Portal was called. Fair and stalwart, he stepped into the witness-box, and his blue eyes were suffused with a great tenderness as he looked at the still figure of the woman he loved.

She stirred and raised her head, like a flower on the slender white column of her neck. Their eyes were mutually questioning for a moment, but strangely enough, in that fraction of time, the tale was told between them. The old, old tale of a man's love for a maid, and of a woman's discovery of her own trembling helplessness—the love that comes suddenly and renders her weak.

She had been thinking a great deal of Alec Portal during these last four agonising months. Somehow he had persisted in her thoughts. She had grown instinctively to rely on him. When all else failed—when despair and misery, terror and horror held her in their grip during the silent watches of the night, she had often shaken them off by thinking of that fair, grim face with the steel-blue eyes. The face of a faithful friend. One who was a fighter.

And a lover!

It came to her suddenly in a flash from his blue eyes, the

message of a man's fine clean love and adoration. And ere she could control her own emotion, her confusion had betrayed her too. With the blood mantling her face like a flame, she cast her eyes down. But to the wild beating of her heart an inner voice sang an old, old song that once she had sang for him at the piano, and which he had rather liked. Strange that it should come back to her now!

'Love holds the key to set me free,
And love will find a way.'

Both were unconscious that a man was leaning forward in his seat in the well of the court, tense, held in thrall, the only one indeed, who had discerned the little by-play between them. And it had come to Derek Capel like a physical shock. He stared at them with hands clenching and unclenching, his breath coming hard between his teeth. He had lost again. Of a truth he was fortune's fool and plaything. Though he loved her dearly, she did not love him—never had loved him. All her love was given to this other man.

Then, indeed, the hopeless, bleak look settled in Derek Capel's eyes, and he became a lost man. His wealth, good name, the beautiful old home of Capel Manor—what were they without her by his side to share them? He sat back with folded arms, watching them, a prey to the blackest despair. No good trying to face it out. He took the cup of bitterness and drained it to its dregs.

He scarce took any heed as the procedure of the court went on. Sick at heart, he would have got up and lurched out—left it all behind him, but that he knew he would not be permitted to interrupt at such a stage.

For Alec Portal was giving his evidence, and he spoke in a quiet, authoritative tone that impressed judge and jury alike.

'Will you tell us what you know of the relations existing between deceased and his wife?' asked counsel for the defence.

'They were unhappy,' said the young doctor gravely. 'Professor Appleby was a man of brilliant but perverted gifts. His discoveries in the cause of science bear witness to his amazing genius. But I must speak of the warped side of his nature, of which the world knows little. He was a man with a twisted heart, a man who delighted in evil, and worked it for its own sake.

'In certain moods,' went on Doctor Portal, 'he came very near the border-line of insanity. I have seen him in such moods, and I knew him to be positively dangerous. His greatest obsession was a hatred of physical beauty in women. And he had married a young and beautiful wife.'

In the pause that ensued, all eyes were turned on the exquisite face of the woman in the dock, with the great brown eyes darkened now by the violet shadows suffering had cast. The terrific strain gave way suddenly, and Eleanor covered her face with her hands, her slim body becoming shaken by sobs.

'He was cruel to her,' Doctor Alec Portal went on. 'Subtly, hideously cruel. He brought her to a state of nervous exhaustion.' And he proceeded to tell of his professional visit to Professor Appleby's wife on the afternoon of the twenty-sixth, his concern at her obvious condition of nervous excitement and fear, and of his straight-forward warning to the professor that had resulted in him being ordered from the house.

'Do you think,' asked counsel, 'that she might have been goaded to such a condition of mind as to plot and carry out her husband's death?'

'Emphatically not,' answered Doctor Portal in a firm voice that rang through the court. 'She was in a state of childish and helpless fear. She was like an innocent child in the hands of King Herod. Such people cannot plot and carry out murders.'

This almost ended the doctor's evidence for the defence. That it carried weight with Justice Horlinge and the jury could not be gainsaid. It had been delivered with a straightforward earnestness and manliness that held the whole court in thrall, though it was recognised that it had been a pleading for the defence, rather than the evidence of facts elicited from cross-examination.

One more question David Greatorex asked.

'What is your opinion, as a medical man, of the manner in which Professor Appleby met his death?'

'I have not been allowed to examine the body, though I asked to do so,' answered the doctor coldly. 'From my own observations, however, I should not be surprised if the professor died in an epileptic fit.'

Then he retired from the witness-box.

Eleanor was next called, and she told her story in low, sweet tones that thrilled the court. Unnaturally calm and wonderfully beautiful in sublime surrender to her fate, it was not strange that every heart beat faster when upon the ears of the assembly in court fell the clear, sweet, indescribably mournful voice.

She told the miserable, sordid story of her married life, of her constant and growing fear of her husband, and then of the fits of giddiness, the paling and trembling that had urged her to call in the aid of Doctor Portal.

When, however, she came to the events of that fateful night, she fell, as before, to faltering. The assembly in court hung on her words painfully. The hectic flush that stained her cheeks and then left them woefully pale; the frightened eyes that would never look directly at anyone; the marked hesitance to answer questions—all those produced a disturbing impression which it was difficult to shake off. It was as if she had some guilty knowledge of that night which she was endeavouring to conceal.

'I—I had retired to my bedroom when Mr Capel called late that night,' she said in low, scarcely audible tones. 'He was not expected. My husband sent a maid to call me down to help to entertain him . . . Yes; I was fully dressed at that time.'

'For what reason did you retire again before your guest had left?' asked Sir Hugo Rattenbury inexorably.

'I—my husband ordered me to go,' she faltered.

'Ordered you to go!' repeated counsel sharply. 'A man does not shame his wife without provocation. There was some reason for this, surely. Come, tell the court.'

'There—I—he just did things like that,' she said desperately.

Sir Hugo Rattenbury peered at her through his glasses. 'I suggest there was a reason,' he said sternly. 'It was that your husband had reason to be jealous of your intimacy with Mr Capel.'

'He had no reason,' she cried in a sudden, clear, ringing voice. 'As God is my witness, he had no cause to suspect me of being other than a faithful, if useless wife.'

Sir Hugo looked down at his papers.

'You retired to your room, and this time undressed and went to bed? You did not go to sleep? No; you lay listening. You say that after quarter of an hour you heard Mr Capel go to the front door, and the professor with him. They stood talking there for perhaps three minutes. During that time you will admit you had an opportunity to slip down into the study?'

'I—I suppose so,' she said, looking round her fearfully. 'But I didn't,' she added on a sudden note of anguish. 'Oh, won't you believe me—I didn't do it.'

'The jury have to sift the evidence before them,' said eminent counsel grimly. 'You have told them that earlier in the evening you came down surreptitiously from your room and witnessed the conversation between the deceased and the late witness, Vera Cummings. I put it to you that, outraged by what you heard then, you stole down again later to the study and placed a certain poison in the port decanter?'

David Greatorex rose at once. 'I protest, your lordship!' he cried. 'If my learned friend wishes to put such a fantastic hypothesis before the court, he should do so in his final speech. It is most irregular. There is not a tittle of evidence to support this absurd theory.'

'I submit that there is,' Sir Hugo Rattenbury said stiffly. 'The maid, Vera Cummings, has said that after Mr Capel had gone she heard the stairs creaking, as if someone were softly creeping up and down.'

'After this same witness had declared that she slept during this period, and had been proved a liar!' declared counsel for the defence scornfully.

His lordship, however, looked up, and in his even tones allowed the question to stand. The respite, however, had served somewhat to cover Eleanor's painful confusion, and counsel for the defence seated himself, hoping that she had nerved herself for the final ordeal.

'And now,' said Sir Hugo Rattenbury deliberately, 'please tell us what you found when, upon being roused by the smashing of the vase, you came down into the study.'

'I found him sitting huddled in the chair,' she gasped. 'He was groaning terribly. I—I didn't know what to do. And then the others came.'

'You were standing by the table bearing the decanters, clutching at the heavy plush curtain. You were trembling, scarce able to support yourself. What made you relinquish your grasp of the curtain and take up the port decanter?'

'I—I—' she looked wildly round. 'I don't know.'

'Come, come. Mr Capel asked for a drink, did he not?'

'I—I don't remember.'

'And before he could pour it out you snatched the decanter again and allowed it to slip from your grasp. I suggest that you did that wilfully, with the full knowledge that if Mr Capel had drunk from the decanter, he, too, would have been poisoned.'

A moment she looked at him strangely with her large and beautiful brown eyes. It was as if she were in a state of coma, hypnotised by that suggestion. Then slowly a terribly hunted look crept into her eyes, and trembling visibly, she clutched at the rails of the witness-box, shaking her head.

'You knew,' counsel accused her, with a terrific venom now in his tongue and look. 'You knew that the decanter contained poison. You had poisoned your husband, and you did not wish to poison the man you loved. Come, tell the truth.'

It was the supreme moment. She was beaten down, with all the spirit gone from her. She had passed through a frightful ordeal such as might have broken the spirit of the hardiest and caused reason to rock. Even those in the court who believed her guilty—and there were many there!—watched her in tense anxiety. But all at once, after a slight fit of shuddering, she raised her head proudly and uplifted her arms with a strange, rapt splendour in her eyes.

'Heaven hear me,' she cried, in a clear voice that thrilled the court, 'I had no knowledge of any noxious or poisonous contents of the decanter. Alone in the world, reviled, wrecked for all time, without a ray of hope, I, Eleanor Appleby, deny every accusation brought against me in this cruel arraignment. I am innocent! Innocent! Thou, God, knowest! Innocent of this sin, as the angels that see thy face.'

And then, with a little choking cry, she collapsed.

Hardly able to conceal his disappointment, Sir Hugo Rattenbury intimated that he had no further questions to ask. The case was marching swiftly to its conclusion now, for counsel for the defence did not wish to examine prisoner at the bar, and an adjournment was ordered for lunch.

After the luncheon interval, David Greatorex, K.C., rose to his feet to make his final speech for the defence. It was a marvellous piece of oratory, impassioned and skilful, lasting for two hours. It can be read by the curious today who seek among the blue books of the Record Office, and even in cold print it stands as a fascinating and moving exposition of the forensic art. How much more moving was it when delivered by Mr Greatorex himself to a hushed and breathless court? His was a personality that could hold audiences spell-bound and sway emotions as the wind the full-blown corn. Those in court stared at the gaunt figure with its enveloping gown, the keen, ascetic face with the dark eyes aglow, as if at a prophet, and they listened with a tingling shiver to the voice that rang like a bugle call:

'Gentlemen of the jury, what madness does the law perpetrate, what hideous injustice in asking you judicially to murder this innocent and pure-hearted woman? I am astounded. You have heard the facts—the dark array of facts that the prosecution have brought before you. After subjecting this young and sensitive girl to months of unspeakable agony and torture, they have arraigned her before the bar of Justice on a charge of murdering her husband—and they cannot tell you how he died!

'It is a monstrous thing,' went on the advocate passionately. 'It is a blunder so frightful that it borders on as heinous a crime as that for which their victim stands arraigned. Consider it, gentlemen of the jury. An autopsy has been made on the body of the deceased by the most clever pathologists in the world, and all they can say is that there is evidence of poisoning, and that they suspect a subtle and little known poison that will give evidence of its presence in the organs after a period of time has elapsed. For shame! Upon that risky prognostication to hustle a young and innocent life beyond the Great Divide!

'What else is outstanding amongst this dark array of facts that confronts you, gentlemen of the jury? The Crown have pinned all their faith upon the accused's breaking of the port decanter. They have analysed the pool on the floor and discovered no poison in it. You have had evidence to show that there were two glasses in the study stained with port after the professor's death, and the ether person, Mr Derek Capel, who drank from one of the glasses, is not dead. Do you for one moment give credence to this ridiculous theory that the professor's port had been poisoned?'

Counsel for the defence went on to argue most eloquently that the professor's glass of port, already poured out, might have been poisoned by accused rather than the decanter. What then was the object of smashing the decanter?

He dealt at great length with Doctor Alec Portal's evidence,

adducing it as eminently reliable. The deceased was a man of
brilliant gifts, who dealt in vivisection, anthropology and other
sciences that were essentially of a cruel nature. Whether his
studies preyed on his mind or not, he was certainly a victim of
incipient insanity. Might he not have taken his own life? He
was versed in poisons. He hated his wife, and with the cunning
of an insane person, he might have planned this fearful aftermath
of his death—the trial of his wife for murder.

David Greatorex then proceeded to deal scornfully with the
evidence of Vera, the house palour-maid. She was an utterly
untrustworthy witness, a liar, schemer, and the mistress of
Professor Appleby in his own home. Counsel hinted that her
own conduct might, with advantage, be investigated by the
police. Was she above suspicion—this woman who had tried
to brand an innocent young wife with the mark of Cain?

'Gentlemen of the jury, I do earnestly appeal to you to be
guided by reason when you retire to consider your verdict.
do not ask for compassion for the prisoner. It is too late for
that now. I do not ask you to consider her youth, her obvious
helplessness and guilelessness, nor the life of suffering she has
endured at the mercy of the deceased. I ask you—nay, I demand
from you, twelve good men and true,' said David Greatorex
thumping the table, 'that you, selected for your intelligence and
impartiality, who have patiently and attentively listened to the
evidence in the case, do now swiftly and decisively reject the
trumped-up evidence against this fair and innocent woman. .
ask you to acquit her of this monstrous and iniquitous charge
so that she may leave the court a free woman and without a
stain upon her character.'

And David Greatorex sat down, his face shining with his
own belief and sincerity.

An astonishing and sensational thing happened then. The
jurors were seen to whisper and confer amongst themselves,
and then the foreman rose, and after signing and whispering
to the clerk of the court, who conveyed a message to the judge

he faced his lordship, who sat gravely expectant, while a stillness
of death fell upon the court.

The foreman spoke, emotion writ large upon his face, and
his voice a little tremulous.

'We, the jury, in this case of the Crown against Eleanor
Appleby, do wish to stop this case, not desiring to hear any
further evidence in the indictment for or against the accused.'

'I understand,' said his lordship gravely. 'Then, gentlemen
of the jury, you have already considered your verdict? And you
are agreed upon it?'

'We are,' replied the foreman.

'What say you? Guilty or not guilty?'

'We find the prisoner not guilty,' came the answer in an
emotional voice, 'and we wish to add a rider that we consider
his indictment against Mrs Appleby should never have been
brought.'

'Not guilty!'

Cheers rang through the court. The tension was at last
relaxed, and for a few moments most unseemly disorder reigned.
Women wept openly, and men laughed and spoke to one another
with delight. It was some moments before the ushers' voices
and the judge's stern reprimand quelled the audible expression
of the compassionate sympathy and gladness that flowed
through the court at the verdict.

Then the judge spoke.

'Eleanor Appleby, the jury, in conscientious discharge of their
duty, have sought to end your suspense by respectfully begging
that this trial shall be stopped. Without retiring to consider
their verdict, they acquit you of the indictment against you.
Their verdict of "not guilty" is one with which I entirely agree,
and I am bound to say that I endorse their rider that the charge
should never have been brought. You are therefore entitled to
leave this court at once, a free woman, with honour untarnished
and without a stain upon your character.'

And his lordship actually beamed upon her.

A minute afterwards, however, he was compelled to give an order to clear the court, so great was the enthusiasm at the result. Even Alec Portal was unable to curb his joy and gladness. He rose from his seat and made his way to the well of the court, where he waved his hand to Eleanor delightedly.

She smiled wanly at him as she was led out of the dock by a motherly wardress. Never had she appeared so beautiful in his eyes. A tiny, hectic spot of colour stained the pallor of her cheeks as she looked at him, lashes tremulous, lips aquiver in that smile. She seemed to him a girl again—the spirit of girlhood incarnate. Yet a woman to love, to cherish and worship.

She was gone. But he would see her again outside the court. He would take her away to a land of sunshine and flowers. Their honeymoon, by gad! He laughed joyously at the thought. Where should they spend it? In Naples? In Rome? In the Mediterranean of sapphire-blue seas and skies? Or in sunny Havana, mecca of the millionaires, where the lofty, slender, smooth-skinned palms give a romantic grace to every skyline, where all is sweet music in that exotic, dreamy, curious island. Yes; there she might learn to forget.

Whilst he strode from the court, reckless and tingling with the consciousness of this great love that had come to him, another man stood staring into space. It was Derek Capel, unconsciously twirling that tiny moustache of his, yet with all the debonair, reckless charm eradicated from his face now. He looked haggard and worn; almost seedy. A policeman came along, and none too politely ushered the abstracted loiterer out of the court.

Derek went outside like a man in a dream. A spasm crossed his face, of mingled gladness and pain. She was free! Free! Thank Heaven for that. But—

Oh, he had seen the look she had given Alec Portal. Hopelessly, passionately in love himself, he was keenly intuitive in these matters. And he knew that his cause was lost.

Eleanor loved this other man. The thought drummed

nsistently in his brain. He had seen it in her shy smile, in the ook she gave him even in that moment when the relief from he strain and suspense of months must have had an over-vhelming effect on her. And he had dared to hope all this time, o think . . .

He stopped in the middle of the pavement. A surge of ungovrnable, murderous passion shook his whole being. His andsome face was distorted, scarcely nice to look at.

'Oh, blast!' he said aloud, very bitterly.

So he wrestled with his demons as he trudged on with his ands in his overcoat pockets. He furiously repelled that insidous, murderous thought that had come to him . . . that awful hought in connection with Doctor Alec Portal.

No; the game had been played. He had lost. He must be an conoclast—destroy the sweet image of the girl that was in his eart and brain. The only way to do that was to seek other listractions.

A newsboy came running at full tilt, crying his wares—that ry of 'Piper! Late edishun!' that is peculiar to London. He was loing a roaring trade. Derek Capel stopped and stared down he wet, shining pavements after him. The newsboy carried a ill bearing the words:

MRS APPLEBY: TRIAL VERDICT!

Derek Capel's face worked strangely. Could he never get way from it all.

. . . All at once he saw the frosted glass of a public-house, nd he went in, out of the drizzling rain.

And Alec? He waited at a side entrance of the Old Bailey om which he knew she would emerge, his clear-cut face very oyish and his eyes lit with that tender, exultant glow that comes eldom to a man. So he stood, tall and well groomed, pawing t the ground with his cane, while he gave his thoughts full ein. There seemed some magic in the air this chilly, wet

November afternoon. His blood was turned to fire, consuming him. He was the eager, ardent lover—burning to see her.

He turned restlessly, oppressed by something, he knew not what. Was it this building of steel and stone that still seemed to hold her prisoner. Why did she not come? He would soon take her away from this chilly, foggy London in November.

Even then he did not see them; he was not properly sensible of them—those figures, grotesque, umbrella-clad, that thronged the opposite pavement, only held in leash by burly, impatient constables. They were the passers-by, the curious sightseers. the moving and component parts of London's phantasmagoria—call them what you will. They throng to a hole dug in the ground by workmen; they press with morbid eagerness to the scene of an accident. Like weeds, they are not to be checked.

But Alec, with the eyes of a lover searching only for one object, did not see these monstrous shadowy figures that hung expectant under London's growing pall of dusk.

Lighting-up time! She came out at last with the lights, whose glowing reflections danced on the wet pavements. A coat with silver-gray fur, like Columbine's ruffles at neck and wrists, garbed her slimly. Alec jerked forward with London's roar dying to sweet, subdued music in his ears. How pretty she was—how pretty!

'Eleanor!' Her name broke from his lips like a sob of happiness. 'Oh, my dear . . . I thought you were never coming. I've been thinking awful thoughts—almost making up my mind to break in there and carry you away. But you are free! Free!' He stopped suddenly, the wild song of gladness that had been welling in his heart dying—giving place to a queer dread.

For she was looking at him with those great, lovely eyes of hers, and they were haunted by fear unnameable.

She was looking past him wildly. She wanted to escape. And when he barred her path, perplexed and hurt, she covered her face with her little gloved hands and burst into tears.

He laid light hands on her arm. 'Eleanor—look at me! Has anything happened? . . . Tell me, dear heart.'

But the next moment he knew, and inwardly he cursed them savagely as they broke the police cordon across the road and came rushing to see—those curious sightseers. Of course! He had forgotten that she was the beautiful Mrs Appleby, heroine of the latest and most sensational murder trial. He cursed himself as stark reality came back to him. He had been too precipitate. Stupid fool that he was—always blundering.

Girls pressed forward with autograph albums and pencils; there was the vivid flash that accompanies a camera exposure, and an untidy journalist working for one of the big London 'dailies' was endeavouring to persuade Eleanor to come to his office with him in a taxi, where a fat cheque awaited her in return for an exclusive interview with photographs.

Eleanor was frightened, pitiably frightened. Now she clung to Alec Portal, her little gloved hand plucking at one of the buttons of his coat, her eyes dewed with tears.

'Oh, can't you see?' she gasped, 'They're staring! They're all staring at me! Take me away from here—please, or I shall die of shame!'

Something like an oath was wrenched from his lips.

He glared at the eager throng that pressed around them, but for a moment he was oppressed by a sense of futility. All at once, however, he saw a big car, whose interior was lighted, and, desperate for the woman he loved, he raised his stick to signal to it. As if the driver anticipated his wishes, the long low car swung up to the kerb, and a man pushed open one of the doors hurriedly and jumped out on to the pavement, obviously holding the door wide for them and looking over towards them.

It was Chief Inspector Brent of Scotland Yard, his grizzled face somehow softened as he looked at the woman whom he had been chiefly instrumental in placing on trial for her life.

'In here,' he said, gruffly enough.

Alec Portal, with a surge of relief, piloted Eleanor towards the waiting motor-car, his hand on her elbow. Even at that moment, distracted as he was by the vulgar crowd, he knew a thrill that was akin to pain at the mere touch of her; her close proximity. A mad elixir seemed to run through his veins. Heavens, he loved her—loved her!

She was seated in the car and he beside her, and they were being whirled away.

Inspector Brent seemed to have foreknowledge of her intentions and wishes. He sat in a seat in front like a graven image, occasionally directing the uniformed driver; and the car swept on, through Euston's broad thoroughfare, Tottenham Court Road, and towards the great terminus of Paddington station.

Alec Portal had sat silent for some time, a feeling of unease growing on him. She seemed so defenceless, so alone in the world, that he yearned to take her in his arms, to tell her of his love.

And yet—there was some barrier between them; intangible, yet definite enough to chill his ardour. Scarcely was it the barrier of her shyness and reserve; so great was his love for her that he felt he might have surmounted that . . .

He turned restlessly.

He was almost afraid of himself, frightened of his own desires and thoughts and secret longings.

What a divine, sweet, intoxicating little thing she was. And she was free—free to become his wife! She must love him too, he thought fiercely. He could feel it—he knew it! They were made for each other.

She sat in the corner, her face half averted from him, stained with tears. He thought of some crushed, beautiful flower as he looked at her. And he longed savagely to take her in his arms. But then, like a cold douche, came remembrance of those hours of cross-examination, questioning, as she had stood in the dock under the pitiless gaze of the curious. The acid had been poured on her to test her. The cold white light of inquiry had flooded on her. It had served only to discover that she was innocent and pure. Yet it must have seared her. She was afraid—trembling—utterly unnerved. Afraid to face the curious gaze of the world! He as a doctor should have known that. He lashed himself all at once with thoughts of his own callousness. What a brute—a callous brute he was—to impose his wooing upon her at this time!

Despite it all, as he stared at her he became unnerved, weak as any man might be.

'Eleanor?' he whispered huskily.

She turned to him with a start, mutely, her eyes questioning him in fear. And something he saw in the depths of those lovely brown eyes wrung at his heart. She was afraid of him too!

There was a barrier between them; a barrier, almost sinister, that had arisen out of the past.

A silence that was constrained fell between them.

'Do you hate me then?' he asked desperately at last, in a strained voice. 'Eleanor, I love you. I've tried so hard to help.' He edged a little nearer. 'Little girl, it hurts me—that broken look!'

A tiny gasp and a sob escaped her, but he succeeded in gaining her hand.

'Eleanor—why fret about the past? It's all over now, and what is the world to you and me? We'll go away—forget it all. Sweetheart; won't you let me come to you—to woo you as a man would his only love?'

'I'm going away,' she said in a very small and distant voice. Actually she was struggling desperately for control.

'I know,' he said a little wildly. 'You are going away. Where? Where are you going? Oh, my love; something seems to tell me that if you go it will be a very, very long time before I see you again.'

After a pause he added more gently: 'Forgive me. You are overwrought. I recognise that. In decency I should leave you to yourself until you have got over this. Time may heal. And in the meantime,' he added bitterly. 'I am a cad. An insufferable cad to press you. But, oh, my dear—Eleanor!—something impels me to speak . . .'

Eleanor did not turn her head, but the passionate, pleading

voice caused her heart to leap madly in her bosom. She loved him. Heaven help her! All her thoughts were of this new ardent lover, whilst in the gray sprawling city around her fair name and reputation was being spiced and mixed till it became a veritable concoction of scandal.

She tried to shake it off—that haunting terror of publicity and scandal that to the sensitive and refined is far more to be shunned than the yawning pit.

And for a moment, as she looked at him, she forgot it all. She saw and remembered only him. Despite herself, in spite of all her resolutions, words flooded up to her lips and made her answer him.

'Alec, don't—speak like that,' she said, low and huskily. 'You don't know—oh, you don't know how I care!'

He turned to stare at her, his face dark and fierce, almost hawk-like. But then it seemed that the question he silently asked her was answered, for he bowed his head and there was joy and humility in his face.

'Sweetheart, forgive me,' he whispered. 'I wait and hope, darling heart. One day you will send for me, and I shall come, and I shall know from your dear eyes, and I shall say "Let's get married," and you will say, "Yes."' He laughed huskily and joyously. 'You will send for me, Eleanor?'

She shivered, and with almost a maternal gesture she stretched out her ungloved hand and touched his fair hair. She was knowing now for the first time, and to the full, the beauty and mystery, the mingled pain and glory of love and all that love means to a woman.

'My lover,' she murmured with infinite compassion. 'Alec, heart of mine, I feel it too—that nothing but sorrow can come from this love of ours. Yet—oh, I don't know! If I can forget the other thing, I feel I must send for you one day. I—I'm going abroad, Alec.'

He did not ask her where. He remained silent, respecting her unspoken wishes.

'Alec, you are a true lover,' she murmured. 'You have come
a-wooing as a woman would have it.' She paused breathlessly
a moment. 'You could have been so cruel to me. For I love you,
and if you had persisted at this moment—I am too weak to
resist. But you are of finer clay than that, Alec. You will give
me time . . .?'

He had not time to say anything, for the big lighted car was
swooping down into Paddington Station. But he knew misery
as it came to a standstill, and Inspector Brent, jumping down
from his seat beside the chauffeur, opened the door for her.

A maid was waiting for Mrs Appleby. Apparently her luggage
had been put on the boat train for Dieppe, and now she was
being led to a saloon carriage.

Alec Portal trailed after the little procession. A station official
was fussing round Eleanor, and it was evident that whatever
notoriety had preceded her she had acquired a new importance
in the station official's eyes as an elegant and beautiful woman.
She did, indeed, seem to symbolise life itself as she stepped
into the waiting carriage—life and joyous youth. One forgot the
marble white face and saw only the lissom form, the ravishing
profile, the slim, silken-clad ankles. 'Midst all this bustle of
Continental travel she seemed to stand out as the one girl for
whom it had all been invented—the one breathless girl!

Alec Portal pressed forward with a stabbing pain at his heart.
How different from his dreams! Then they had been going away
together! And he could not now press near enough to say one
last word to her.

Time was getting short, and it was the taciturn, uncompro-
mising Inspector Brent who had the last words with her. With
a flush creeping into his grizzled face, he held out a hand to
where she sat ensconced amongst flowers, chocolates and
magazines.

'Good-bye, madam'—gruffly. 'I hope you have a pleasant
recuperation. 'Gainst my usual practice, coming like this. I felt
I must apologise—for—everything!'

Eleanor understood, and she put her hand into his with mute sympathy. He went on gruffly enough:

'I did what I thought was my duty, madam. I committed a heinous blunder that I shall remember to my dying day. I know I was wrong, and I want to say that there is no more staunch believer in you than I am now.'

'But,' he added, with a weary shake of his head. 'I should like to get to the bottom of the mystery. I'd take fresh lines of investigation, only—' He paused. 'I've got a feeling that one day I shall learn the truth.'

But now the train was on the move.

Alec Portal watched it with an aching heart, though he waved his hat and tried to smile. Inspector Brent stood back as it went out, with a commiserating shake of his head. He little guessed then of the startling manner in which his half prophecy of 'learning the truth one day' was to be fulfilled.

CHAPTER VII

LEFT alone in the private saloon carriage of the boat train, Eleanor knew the misery of loneliness and began to feel an intolerable heartache. She put up her hand, with the back of her wrist to her burning eyes. The thought that she would not see him again, that she loved him and they were being wider separated every moment by the thundering wheels of the train, overcame her and she burst into tears.

It is probable that the frailer sex have done this since the time of Eve. To a woman there must at some time come the sweet sorrow of parting, and tears are Nature's balm to soften the heartache. Tears! A myriad have been shed for every glittering light on Broadway or Piccadilly, and mayhap they shall form the cascade of cleansing as each of us pass into that other world.

But Eleanor's fit of crying was so violent and prolonged that in the end it frightened even herself. She tried frantically to calm herself, to check the choking sobs that came from her lips. These tears were no solace; they were the frightened cries of a creature lost in the wilderness.

At length, with her handkerchief at her lips, she forcibly checked her sobbing. She looked at her pretty face in the mirror of her bag, and told herself it was a ruin. There came those little adjustments with powder puff that even the best and most discreet of women indulge in nowadays. She was trying to put up a brave fight.

She made up her mind to take tea in the dining-car of the train, tea being the panacea for a good many ills. And to see the people around her would prove some distraction.

She rose, gathering up feminine trifles. But suddenly a sob shook her slender frame. She realised with something akin to panic that they were almost uncontrollable. Her heart was crying out to Alec—beseeching him to come to her.

It was then that Fate, or Fortune—call it what you will—played one of its most devastating tricks upon one whom, until now, it had treated none too kindly. For Eleanor, seeking distraction, desperately gathered up chocolates and a magazine and hastened into the dining-car.

She might have taken tea in the privacy of her own saloon carriage, for no expense had been spared on this trip. As it was she sat down at a table, only to incur curious recognition from the eyes of a fair-haired girl who sat at a table opposite.

This girl was Violet Delamere, an actress. And she flitted into Eleanor Appleby's life and out again all in a moment. Yet she played a most amazing part in it.

Violet Delamere was possessed of a personal reputation as dubious as the authenticity of her name. The first blush of her youth was gone, though she was still a pretty woman. Hotel proprietors, tradesmen and the like, withdrew swiftly into their shells of reserve when she was mentioned, for the 'high sign' had been given about this pretty confidence trickster. Not to be too flippant, she was 'that kind of a woman,' and she was known in every gay capital, except Vienna, where she proposed to journey now for the sake of her health.

She studied Eleanor covertly under lowered lashes. A newspaper lay by Violet Delamere's side even now, containing 'glare lines' announcing 'Mrs Appleby's Acquittal,' together with a large photograph under which the caption writer had lavished phrases concerning 'this tragic and beautiful woman.'

The fair adventuress knew all about her, and she swiftly decided that Eleanor was in no fit condition to look after herself. Her slender frame trembled visibly, and at moments her beautiful face was expressive of the horror she had recently undergone. She endeavoured to maintain a steadfast gaze out of the window at the moving scenery, but it was evident that her mind was a whirl of chaotic thoughts and memories.

Violet Delamere swiftly decided a more important point for herself; that Eleanor was not capable of looking after her own property. Her bag lay on the seat by her side, and there was not waiter, or anybody else, near at hand. So Violet Delamere leisurely finished her tea, and having paid her bill, rose to leave the dining-saloon.

She lurched as if with a movement of the train as she passed Eleanor's table, and murmured a low-voiced apology, which was hardly noticed. Much less did Eleanor notice the absence of her bag immediately after. The adventuress had obtained possession of it very skilfully, and she retired to an empty carriage to investigate, the spoil.

She found in the bag currency notes and banknotes, which she desired. And she also found a sheaf of letters, one or two of which Eleanor had received quite recently in reply to her own. Three of these were from the Mother Superior of St Augustine's Convent near Caldilly, in France, where Eleanor as a girl had received her education. They told the adventuress of Eleanor's intentions, for they were sweet, kindly letters, welcoming the much-tried girl back to the convent.

Violet Delamere read the letters, and had one of her 'marvellous inspirations.' This other woman, who had attained the blaze of notoriety through a public trial for murder, was retiring from the world into a convent, whereas she, Violet Delamere, had her way to make in the world.

She could dance and she could sing. And she knew the value of a notorious name in the Vienna cabarets. They would welcome with open arms the beautiful Eleanor Appleby who had suffered so much, and yet who could be so gay.

Violet Delamere smiled as she tore the letters and threw them with the bag out of the carriage window. She had determined to become the beautiful Mrs Appleby in Vienna, and play the game for all it was worth.

*

To Eleanor it seemed that Fate had surely set its frowning face against her when eventually she discovered the loss of her bag. It contained a great deal of money, but she was too heartbroken to inform the authorities. She had just enough money to see her through, and so on landing she took the train to Caldilly, and set out distractedly to walk the remainder of her journey to the convent.

She had almost made up her mind as to her future life. In twelve months, after her novitiate stage was passed, she would take the veil and become a nun.

It was a delightful evening for a walk, and the country lane seemed inviting. The breeze was stirring in the orchard on either side, relieving the apple trees of some of their burden. The russet and gold windfalls were dropping softly in the dewy grass, there to lie like jewels.

But Eleanor, walking with weary, dogged steps, did not seem to appreciate the beauty of the evening. She looked up at the stars and sighed. Everything seemed to be out with her mood.

'Alec!' she cried miserably at length. 'Oh, Alec!'

As the cry left her lips she stopped, and then quickened her pace again, trying to banish him from her thoughts. But despite herself, thoughts of him, his little tricks of speech and manner, would—simply would—insistently hammer at her brain.

She looked ill and worn. Her small oval face had an unnatural pallor, and her eyes were hard and strained. At moments, as some particular recollection was brought back to her, her lips would twitch painfully.

Hardly did she know where she was walking, until at length, looking around her drearily enough, she found herself in the little village of Caldilly itself, with the convent of St Augustine's not far distant.

Then all at once fear caught at her throat as she thought again of what she contemplated. The convent walls; the chaste life of a nun! There would be none to know of her passing from the world except those within the gates of St Augustine's. But out here in the world were love and laughter and gaiety. The bubbling effervescence that is life. And she was so young and made to enjoy it all.

Then she told herself drearily that life had little to give to her . . . Except, perhaps—Alec!

The thought of him was like a pang. Looking around her, she saw the twinkling lights of the village post office, which she recognised, and a sudden resolution came to her to write to him. She would not have the letter posted at once. She needed time, rest—time to adjust her ideas of life. But once within the convent walls, and started upon her novitiate stage, she knew that the strict rules would not permit her to write many letters to those in the outside world. Her letters would be read by the Mother Superior.

With a jerk she started towards the little village post office.

The kindly old postmaster, who had known her when St Augustine's was a girls' convent school, not as it was now, a shelter for the Sisters of Mercy only, received her with glad surprise and welcome. He readily acceded to her request that she might write a letter there, and also that it should be posted after a lapse of months.

It was a pitiful little letter she wrote of a few hasty lines that came from her heart.

'Alec . . . Oh, my dear, I am so lonely and heartbroken! Perhaps you will not want me now, but if you do, come to St Augustine's Convent at Caldilly. If I should never see you again, God keep and cherish you. Lovingly.—Eleanor.'

After it was written and sealed she felt a little lighter in spirit, and she bade her adieux to the kindly old postmaster with a smile curving her lips for the first time for weeks.

She envisioned Alec again as she walked on through the country lanes . . . smiling at her, holding forth his arms to take her. Then all at once she came in sight of St Augustine's Convent, wrapped in darkness and in slumber.

Only one light showed from the stately pile that was now ages old, and it came from the room of the Reverend Mother.

The candles were still burning in that apartment. They sent a fitful gleam through the stained glass window out into the darkness. And inside the sombre room, her sweet face rather sad, sat the Reverend Mother Superior.

Her shapely white hands were clasped over the rosary which hung round her neck, and as she fingered it, she sang softly to herself:

> 'The hours that I spent with thee, dear heart,
> Are as a string of pearls to me.'

She had a wonderful voice, and as she softly sang, her beautiful face looked almost saintly in the candlelight.

She broke off.

'Strange that I should sing that tonight,' she murmured. 'It is a song of the world, not of the convent. I remember that Eleanor used to sing it. It is five years since she left the convent. And now . . .'

Her thoughts lingered round the girl who had once been a pupil at the convent school. Eleanor had been a slender, fair-haired girl with large, expressive eyes and great promise of beauty then. And now she was married, and tragedy had engulfed her.

The Reverend Mother Superior did not read newspapers, yet she had experienced a fairly full knowledge of life, and in the piteous and almost incoherent letters that Eleanor had sent her she had been able to read between the lines.

She read the story of a sensitive girl subjected to subtle mental cruelty by her husband . . . and then the crash—the tragedy of violent death. In its causes the Reverend Mother

Teresa was scarcely as interested as in its effects upon the girl whom she had loved in those old days when she had been a convent pupil.

How had it left Eleanor? Had it made her receptive to the quiet and seclusion of these convent walls, or had it merely made her rebellious and frightened of the world for the time being? The Reverend Mother would dearly have loved to welcome Eleanor as a sister, yet she was large and whole-minded, and she knew of the gradual irk that the convent life can invoke upon a youthful spirit.

That, however, was all in the future. The Reverend Mother was fain to confess to a vague stirring of uneasiness tonight. She had received a letter and later a telegram from Eleanor, saying she was arriving today. And up till now she had not come.

It was late, and the Mother Superior scarcely expected her now until morning. Yet, knowing the uneasy spirit that must possess Eleanor Appleby, she felt afraid.

Just then there came an interruption to her train of thought—a queer sound on the stained glass window.

'Tap, tap!'

The Reverend Mother looked up suddenly. What was it? It sounded as though someone were rapping at her window. But no; it must have been the branch of a tree that knocked against it.

Again it was heard—a quiet but insistent rap. It was not a chance noise, but evidently the summons of someone who wished to attract her attention.

The Reverend Mother rose, and going to the window she opened it and looked out into the darkness.

'Who is there?' she asked in a low voice.

She could just make out a shadowy form—the form of a woman. For a moment there was a tense silence, and then distinctly she heard the sound of a sob.

'Reverend Mother! Oh, please, let me in.'

The Mother Superior started. She knew that voice. It was

the voice of Eleanor Appleby, the girl who a few moments before had been in her thoughts.

'Just a moment,' she said quietly. 'I will come round and unlock the door.'

Hastily she went round to the huge, iron-barred oaken door of the convent, and even while she unlocked it she wondered uneasily at the strange despair that had sounded in the girl's voice.

The door swung open, and Eleanor Appleby came hastily into the passage. The girl's weary, despairing face, the tear-stains under her eyes, and even her mud-stained shoes, all indicated to the Reverend Mother the condition of her mind.

'You look worn out,' said the Mother Superior gently. 'Come into my room.'

In silence they made their way to the sombre, candle-lit room that was the Mother Superior's private apartment; and in silence the Reverend Mother sat down.

What she expected happened. The girl, with a sudden despairing gesture, sank down at the nun's side and buried her face in her lap, giving way to a violent fit of sobbing.

The Reverend Mother softly stroked her fair hair, and looked sadly down at the girl's shapely head. So the world treats those who are beautiful and good and unable to fight against malignant fate! It was useless to say anything while she was in this pent-up condition. The Mother Superior waited until the dry, choking sobs that seemed to rack the girl's whole frame gave place to the relief of tears. She became silent at length, and seemed to grow calmer. Then, and then only, did the nun speak.

'Tell me all about it, dear.'

The girl's pain-stricken eyes in the almost transparent little face were turned on the nun's calm, serene countenance, and for a moment she fought for control to speak.

'Mother,' she whispered huskily, 'I have done wrong. A terrible wrong. Heaven help me—what shall I do?'

She broke off pitifully.

'What do you mean, dear?' The nun asked the question a little sharply. The little imps of fear commenced to play on her nerves as she waited for the answer. It couldn't be— It was impossible to think of any serious wrong in connection with this sweet child!

'I must tell someone,' the girl whispered shamedly. 'Mother, I must confess. It's about me—about—'

She stopped, her face white as death as she lifted it piteously. But somehow she seemed to gain courage from the saintly eyes that looked with infinite compassion down upon her, and in very low and broken tones she made her confession there to the Reverend Mother Superior in the quiet of the candle-lit room.

The nun sat in shocked silence, while the girl talked haltingly, in broken tones. Then at last it was over, and a silence fell. Eleanor buried her face again, while the nun stared before her with eyes that saw nothing. She understood now, and she knew the terrible tragedy that had stamped itself on this girl's mind.

And as the Reverend Mother sat there, she came to her resolution. Weak and sinning though this girl was, she would take her into her fold. She should take the veil, become a nun. To the world outside her confession was as if written in a book that is sealed for evermore. And Eleanor! She had cast her eyes for the last time on the world outside the convent gates.

That was if she wished it; and she had expressed that wish. The Mother Superior had no reason to doubt from her present attitude that she had altered it.

There was a painful pause. Eleanor was staring in front of her as though she saw everything again. And she was trembling violently now.

'Mother, Mother—what shall I do? Speak to me! Say something! Oh, am I so vile in your sight?'

Still the Mother Superior said no word, and Eleanor gradually grew rigid as she knelt there at her knee. She had poured out her confession. At last to one other person she had entrusted the secret that had been so long locked in her heart, that had seemed to be killing her. This silent nun knew of the part she had played in the dreadful happenings of that night.

And she condemned . . .? Righteously she condemned. Yet the Great Teacher has told us that there is no sin that cannot be expiated by remorse and suffering and sorrow. In such coin had Eleanor paid. She would go on paying until the bitter end.

Now her heart was racked with almost intolerable grief and wild, tumultuous pain. She had staked so much on this moment when she might ease the burden of her mind by confession. During the whole of the trial the thought of the quiet convent and the saintly Mother Superior had helped her to bear up, and she had struggled always with this haven in sight.

All along she had told herself she must tell someone—she must! And there was no one else she could tell her secret save the nun. She had hoped for surcease from the strain of it all. For she was one poor sinner who could not support the burden she had to bear . . . And now this—this frozen silence! It was more terrifying than death.

A little gasp came from the suffering woman's lips; still the Mother Superior did not speak.

Eleanor rose to her feet quietly, looking like a wraith. Her face was deathly white, her great brown eyes like pools of fire. There was a vacant intensity in her gaze that instantly frightened the Mother Superior, who roused herself; she had been absorbed in queer, dreadful thoughts.

'I'm going,' Eleanor said; and her usually clear, musical voice had become droning. 'I'm going to tell the police. I can't stand it any longer. It's weighing on my conscience.'

She turned away to the door almost like a somnambulist. Her brown eyes in her deathly white little face were blazing with a strange light.

The Mother Superior rose, and her swishing robes spoke of unusually quick movement as she followed the girl. Almost at the door she caught the slim figure in her arms.

'Eleanor,' she cried in poignant distress, 'would you leave me now? Oh, my poor, poor child—of what are you thinking? What do you contemplate?'

The Mother Superior's anguished, loving tones seemed to move the girl (who had appeared to be almost in a state of trance). Slowly she turned her beautiful, staring eyes on the nun.

'Reverend Mother,' she said, with a heart-tearing sound between a gasp and a sob in her voice, 'I seemed to see a dark pool just then, and there was a spirit hovering over it that seemed to beckon, inviting me, It seemed to tell me that in the pool's dark bosom was my only refuge. I have got to make amends. And—heaven help me!—I cannot go to the police!'

'Why not?' the nun involuntarily cried.

'Because,' the girl cried in a voice that rang like a knell of despair through the sombre room, 'they won't take me. They have told me that I am free—free for all time. They will not try a person twice for murder in England. Oh, heaven, how shall I make amends? Only by the pool . . . the spirit of the pool is calling me.'

'Nay,' whispered the nun, with tears in her eyes as she clasped the girl closer. 'Nay, my child; it is another voice that calls you. He has said "Come unto me all ye that labour and are heavy laden, and I will give you rest." Eleanor, it is another voice that calls you—the voice of the Church.'

She looked at the nun, a great question leaping in her brown eyes. And the Mother Superior tried tremulously to smile. Then suddenly she had the whole weight of the girl in her arms. Eleanor's eyelashes had fluttered down, and with softly expended breath she swooned.

The nun half carried her to a chair and applied restoratives. But as she bent over the girl, gently touching her temples with cool fingers, the Reverend Mother Superior's brain held a whirl of chaotic thoughts.

She looked so innocent—so peaceful and pure, sleeping in oblivion there. And yet—

The nun shuddered and made a valiant effort to dismiss the whole matter from her mind. She had heard of people in a state of trance doing things, committing deeds for which they were not responsible. And afterwards their minds were blank. They had forgotten—or never remembered—those particular actions.

One thing was certain. Eleanor Appleby had been more sinned against than sinning, and if time could heal, if rest and quiet could ease her mind and make her forget the dread past, then the Mother Superior was determined that within the cloisters of St Augustine's Convent Eleanor Appleby's spirit should be healed.

And so it came about. Following her swoon, Eleanor was ill and delirious for many days, but the gentle nursing and care of the nuns pulled her round. Soon her slim figure in simple black might have been seen wandering in the grounds of the convent. Autumn passed to black winter—which became a white winter in January; and the Sisters of Mercy were seen more outside the convent, carrying supplies of food and fuel through the snow to the poor of the village. At long last bleak winter gave place to spring with all its sweet, shy promise. But spite the daffodils and the primroses, the chirrup of birds and the glint of green buds on the trees—despite the seductive soft whispering of the wind, Eleanor did not hear the call of the outer world.

She tended the garden with the nuns, and gave more and more time to her private devotions. Serenity of mind had come to her, and she was preparing to take the veil.

Perhaps she stifled a sigh at the scent of the May blossoms, and at the fluttering freedom of the butterflies. With summer the convent garden became a riot of bloom, and of times a fancy came to her of another such garden as this where once a mere boy in knickerbockers had chased a girl in a gingham frock, and screaming laughter had echoed through the rose bowers and rookeries.

Hide-and-seek in an old-world garden! It had been one of

her earliest memories. Youth—joyous laughter—freedom! Eleanor felt very old and weary as she looked around her and saw the starched white linen and black robes of the nuns through a curtain of tall hollyhocks.

But she was ready. She was nearing the end of her novitiate stage now, and soon would be prepared to take the vows. Ten—eleven—twelve months had gone past. More. She had not counted them after a time.

She thought of Alec Portal, and immediately dismissed him from her mind again as she had schooled herself to do. He had not come; and besides she did not want him to. She had resigned herself to this quiet secluded life in a convent garden where nothing ever seemed to happen and time itself stood still.

The heat was oppressive today . . .

She looked up at the sun, a fierce brazen ball, and then her gaze wandered down to the ground and fixed itself on a little troop of ants scurrying in and out of their hill. Yes; even here in a convent garden the world and Nature were busy. Things lived.

Only she had a heart that was dead within her . . .!

She turned her steps towards her cell with something like a sob in her throat.

CHAPTER VIII

Time slips past remorselessly. When we are very young each day seems an æon of time; for our eyes are strained to glimpse some rosy future. Then the sands of time slip out one by one. When we are older we turn our backs, and work—and we are astonished at the diminishing in the glass when we pause to look. When we are very old, then everything gallops and rushes past us, and, dazed by the mighty problem of life, we wait for everything to become quiet.

Doctor Alec Portal plunged into work. Every illusion had been stripped from before his eyes, and he saw the future as a thing that was smashed. He worked unceasingly day and night. His practice grew larger and more prosperous until he was obliged to employ two doctors as *locum tenens*. The staffs of two great London hospitals that knew him as a colleague watched his progress and predicted a wonderful future for him.

But Alec Portal saw no future for himself. He dared not look into the future—alone.

Work had become a distraction and an anodyne. He worked to still a gnawing pain and hunger. Perhaps he worked so hard also to forget the one letter he had received from Eleanor, and which lay unopened and unread in his desk.

He had received that letter long after the reports had reached him of the notorious Mrs Appleby's activities on the Continent. She was a cabaret dancer in Vienna, he was told. She had a fatal attraction for men, this remarkably beautiful fair-haired woman, who, it was openly stated, had poisoned her husband. There had been many subsequent scandals with which her name was linked.

'Midst all these activities of hers she had found time to send him one letter from France . . .

It is a regrettable fact that human nature is ever more prone to suspicion than to faith. Alec had helped her so much. He had stood by her side and fought the battle with her during the trial. And now—he tried to banish those sweet and tender memories of her; tried not to think of her. If he did, it was certain that suspicion would insidiously creep into his mind and torture him.

Had he been wrong? Given his love and faith to one whom he thought pure and good, and who was in reality . . . a scheming wanton?

He fiercely repudiated the thought. It hurt his self-respect to think that he had been deceived by a beautiful face—those glorious eyes. So complex is the nature of man that he almost forgave what he readily accepted as her subsequent conduct; the wild plunge into gay and riotous living. That was a reaction to the tragic circumstances of her life, he thought.

He should have been by her side to help her—care for her—love her. Things would have been different then. He should have insisted on it.

But that she had deceived him right from the start! Never. It was impossible.

So he tortured himself. And he would not open the letter that had come for him, though it tempted him daily and hourly. He plunged into work to feed his ego, which was the greatest part of him, and so he became, in less than two years, what the world would describe as a successful man.

It was one evening when he was working late in his surgery that Chief Inspector Brent called. Though they still lived as neighbours in the village of Royston, the event of this visit was entirely unprecedented. Indeed, the two men had not seen one another since the trial, and Doctor Portal's eyes gleamed under his fair drawn brows as the Yard man came up the steps and through the little glass house apartment where medicines were placed for callers. He turned the handle of the door and came in like a very tired man to familiar surroundings.

He dropped into a chair with his hat in his hands while Doctor Portal stared an inquiry.

'Good-evening, doctor,' he said, with that heaviness that never left him. And after a pause: 'I'm all wrong again, doctor. This case has worried me since its inception. It was I, you remember, who wrote to you to inform you that Mrs Appleby was performing in a cabaret in Vienna and sent you those foreign newspaper cuttings about her. Well, it's a hoax. A damned hoax. Another woman has been stealing her thunder, as you might say. Masquerading as her.'

'What!'

Alec Portal was visibly galvanised. He crossed to the inspector like a striking hawk and seized him in an iron grip on both shoulders. His fair face was very fierce, and the teeth gleamed above the jutting chin.

'Say that again, you big false alarm!' his voice crackled.

Inspector Brent's eyes were very weary in his heavy but clever face as he lifted them. 'She's in a convent in France,' he explained listlessly, in lieu of repetition. 'Been there for two years. I believe she's becoming a nun. And I've been spreading reports about that little woman,' he added with almost a groan. 'God, the world owes her a lot—'

Alec Portal released him and stood as if he listened to the earth's last tremors.

That letter! And he had never opened it. Fool—mad fool that he had been. To allow carking doubt and suspicion to enter his soul while she . . .

Inspector Brent rose and buttoned his overcoat. Embarrassment made his speech rather stilted and gruff, but he spoke the piece he had come to say.

'You'd better hurry up, young man,' he delivered himself. 'If I was young and in your place, I wouldn't let that little woman become a nun. I'd arrange quite a different religious ceremony. And I don't mean maybe either.'

He drifted towards the door, and out into the night. As he

walked home he sighed more than once. Inspector Brent was a bachelor, and he told himself it was much too late for love to come into his life. In this he was probably right. Besides, the position was positively absurd . . . So Inspector Brent did his best to quench the slumbering fires in his heart.

And Alec? No sooner had the inspector gone than he darted away. Very quickly he had that pitiful little letter in his hands, and was reading it again and again.

'Alex dear,—I am so lonely and heartbroken . . . If you still want me . . . come . . .'

He kissed the letter passionately, and then with shining eyes he looked up. God, he'd go to her—aye, and take her . . . if it was not too late.

At that dread thought he became a whirlwind, so that he aroused the whole of his household. The doctor who was his assistant was obliged to look up the times of the boat trains for him, and his housekeeper looked on horrified while he thrust immaculate suits and shirts haphazard into a travelling case. Never before had anyone seen Doctor Alec Portal so futile in any of his endeavours, and the end of the upheaval witnessed a figure dashing down the steps of the porch into his own car, whilst the chauffeur meshed into gear preparatory to sending the big Studebaker on a sixty mile an hour rush to Southampton.

Alec Portal, however, had a long time for his own thoughts. And any gladness he knew at going to her was tempered by dread. He spent a night tossing and turning. Suppose it was too late. Suppose— Hours he spent conjuring up visions of her, and the dread conviction grew on him that he had lost her.

Comparatively, it seemed like being in heaven when at last the train delivered him at the railway station outside Caldilly. It was just such another night as that on which Eleanor had walked to the convent. The wind sighed through coppice and wood with gentle melancholy, and as the man trudged on he passed the village pond, its waters slightly ruffled, yet almost silvery under the light of the moon, which hung high above like a Chinese lantern in an immeasurable temple of silence.

His mood became queerly fatalistic, and aloud he recited a quaint and entirely melancholy translation from the Chinese of Sao-Nan, whose poems are filled with ineffable sadness:

> 'The moon floats to the bosom of the sky,
> And rests there like a lover;
> The evening wind passes over the lake,
> Touches and passes,
> Kissing the happy, shivering waters.

> 'How serene the joy
> When things that are made for each other
> Meet and are joined.
> But, ah—
> How rarely they meet and are joined,
> The things that are made for each other.'

He laughed suddenly, a little croakily. He was getting morbid. He strode on, a lithe, handsome figure of a man—such a figure, indeed, as might have come from the pages of a romance. And it was a wild and romantic adventure enough, spiced with an indiscretion and recklessness utterly alien to him, that Doctor Alec Portal was to indulge in that night.

He came at last to the walls of the convent, and they were high and grim walls, that cut out any sight of the grounds or the convent itself. There was more than a vague stirring of uneasiness in Doctor Alec Portal's heart as he circumnavigated them—until at last he came to the iron gateway.

He heard the faint and distant sound of a bell tolling, and it increased his uneasiness.

To think that Eleanor was behind those walls, a prisoner!

Virtually a prisoner, for she belonged to the world and to him. She was never made for a nunnery.

Inside the gateway he saw a tiny little house, like a lodge, from which a light glimmered faintly. Also there was an iron bell-knob at the gateway which, he reasoned, connected with the lodge. Coming to a sudden resolution he pulled it, and the bell's clanging within the lodge sounded preternaturally loud and harsh to him.

After what seemed an age, a stately nun appeared and came to the iron bars of the gate. In a low tone Alec Portal stated the purpose of his visit.

'You wish to see her!' the Sister repeated blankly; and then, recovering from her surprise and gathering authority: 'But that is impossible. Quite impossible. She cannot see any visitors.'

Alec was overcome by a sense of futility.

'Why?' he asked desperately. 'Please tell me why.' In despair and dread he added: 'Don't say it is too late!'

The nun looked at him mutely through the bars of the gate, and at his obvious distress, compassion and sympathy fleeted across her face. She seemed to weigh her speech.

'Sir, you had better go your way,' she said at last, kindly enough. 'I do not know the purpose of your visit, but we can let nothing disturb our dear sister now.'

She turned away and disappeared, leaving Alec as if he had been struck a blow.

Perforce, he too moved away from the gateway. Though he was unconscious of it, the tiny beads of sweat stood on his brow, and his soul was pervaded by an anguish of impatience and trepidation. He was confident that something was happening beyond these convent walls—something that was inimical to his love and his hopes of making Eleanor his wife.

It burst upon him with inspiration. The bonds were being forged tonight to fetter her and hold her from him for ever. Even now, it might be, she was taking her vows!

The thought goaded him. It was said of Doctor Alec Portal

amongst the medical profession that he was ever ready to rise to desperate expedients, and now he sustained the character that had been given him. He saw two iron staples in the wall, one above the other, such as are used to hold up ivy, and in a trice he was grappling with the brickwork, climbing the ten-feet wall like a cat.

Breathless and a little dishevelled, he reached the top, cutting his hands on the broken and jagged glass that was cemented along the summit. He essayed the drop on the other side, and landed with a thud that jarred every nerve in his body.

Then he was running through the grounds, wildly, erratically, like a man pursued. His guiding star must have directed him through the maze of carefully tended paths, for he very shortly came in sight of the convent itself . . . and the chapel, its stained glass windows flowing with coloured light, while from within came the soft and awesome strains of the organ.

Alec Portal stopped in the grounds, breathing hard. The sight of this tiny place of worship arrested him a moment, and he swayed in his purpose. Then fear placed its icy clutch on his heart again—fear that he might already have lost her, and he jerked forward towards the chapel.

Within, the strains of the organ were dying to diminuendo. A silence fell upon the strained ears of the man, silence fraught with dread for him. His hands fell on the heavy iron ring of the door, and he turned it.

He burst in. A moment he stood there, scarcely breathing, his eyes dilated as he took in the scene. The solemn awe of it caused his heart to beat as if with hammer strokes. The pews on either side, lined with silent, immobile nuns, their heads bent in prayer; the long aisle richly carpeted; and—Eleanor herself, all in pure white, and looking like a saint as she knelt before the effigy of the Virgin Mary.

'Eleanor!' he called, his voice like a sob of anguish.

The girl kneeling before the altar turned and sprang up, swaying like a lily. For a moment she stared across the empty space at the dark, handsome, reckless face, and then slowly a glorious smile dawned on her tremulous lips.

'Oh, Alec!' she said in a low, rapt voice that yet sounded clearly in that profound silence. 'Alec—my dear! I thought you were not coming. I thought my heart was broken!'

He came to her swiftly then, down the aisle, and with a little gasp she stared at him, and about her, realising the sacrilege of his intrusion upon the scene. But Alec, deeply and fervently religious himself, did not look upon it in this light. He was a man in the sight of God, and to him it seemed a beautiful thing that this girl, to him the most wonderful of all God's creatures, should be given into his care in such a place.

He put his arms about her, but she was trembling violently and her childish face was pitiful.

'Alec—hold me,' she whispered. 'I—here is the Mother Superior.'

The Reverend Mother Superior came down the steps of the altar with stately tread, but there was a wistful, loving smile in her eyes, and faintly upon her lips. She held both her hands out almost as if she would give them her blessing.

'You must go from this place, my children,' she said in low, sweet tones. 'I understand. I should be doing wrong in His sight if I endeavoured to part true love. I will allow you half an hour in the gardens in which to talk and make up your minds. Then the man must go. Eleanor, you will try to weigh in the scales against your love for this man the ideals to which you have already resolved to consecrate your life.'

So they went from the little chapel together, hand in hand, and rather like children they went along the narrow, winding paths . . . until the velvety night swallowed them up. Then he caught her and looked deep into her eyes. It seemed that the question he silently asked her was answered, for he drew her closer, and the eyes that gazed into hers were filled with adoration, humility and gladness.

'Eleanor—oh, Eleanor!' he whispered.

She was shaking, feeling her senses swooning. The translucent light of the slim crescent moon touched her face, crushed against his shoulder; and suddenly something wild and burning, like running fire, flamed through Eleanor, and she put up her little hands to bring down his face to her own.

She gasped at the touch of his lips; it became fierce, hard, relentless pressure, and he strained her quivering figure to his.

The ecstasy of that long, long kiss held Eleanor motionless, enraptured. It was as though he slowly drew her very soul from her. Weak and trembling, and with closed eyes, she lay in his arms, her hands at his heart, and in that moment she surrendered.

Whatever pain and suffering might come to her through this she could bear. She was his—his to love and worship.

Then suddenly she realised that he had relaxed his fierce grip, that he was looking down at her with a world of tenderness in his eyes, humble and contrite.

'Eleanor! Is it so?' he asked huskily. 'Do you really come to me of your own free will?'

'My love,' she answered, with almost a sob. 'Look at me! Am I not in your arms? My heart! . . . feel it . . . how it throbs for you! I come to you gladly—joyfully. Why else?'

He caught her to him again. 'My little girl! My little girl!' he said yearningly. 'I want you. I love you so.'

He kissed her again and again, while she lay palpitating in his arms; her hair, her cheeks, her neck and her mouth he covered with kisses; he held her and kissed her and touched her as he would have touched a beautiful flower.

'Oh, my dear—how beautiful you are!' he whispered huskily. 'I burn for you, when I should kneel at your feet and be glad to live even in the same world that holds you. How queer my love, dear! I feel you to be unattainable—pure, a thing not to be touched. Yet I want to hold you—closer and yet closer.'

She did not answer him in words; with a little smile that seemed to quiver on her lips, she took his head between her hands. With a little exclamation he drew her to him again, so that her breast heaved against his and their hearts beat to the same mad tune, while he took her lips.

She placed a hand on his shoulder at last and smiled at him with a queer sadness in her beautiful eyes. 'My lover!' she murmured with infinite compassion. 'You still love me—and believe. In spite of all that has happened? . . . my name dragged through the mire! Oh, Alex, I was made for tragedy . . . I have a feeling that something awful may happen yet . . . that nothing but sorrow and trouble can come from our love.'

He stared at her, his face dark and earnest.

'Eleanor, we were made for each other; made for love and happiness,' he said. 'There are images in my mind of you; you as a schoolgirl with a pigtail and long legs; you as a sweet maid with the woman in you still slumbering, with only a shy smile and no word for yourself; you as you are now—glorious, divine. And always I've been near, and I've been loving you, Eleanor. I don't know when I found it out, but I've been loving you for years. Now, if this is so, how can anything happen, darling—how can it?'

She clung to him, her little face dewed with tears.

'Alec, dear, dear boy,' she said huskily, 'I shall try to believe that . . . oh, it is silly to think otherwise. Yet I would not hurt you now . . . I would not have you hurt, heart of mine.'

He could not understand. But he was not even vaguely disturbed, for he was so gloriously happy. His arms were around her, and the night gently held the sound of their murmuring voices.

That precious half-hour sped all too quickly. The voice of the Mother Superior was heard at length calling Eleanor, and she parted from her lover with the promise that Alec should see her again with the morning sunshine . . .

Late that night Eleanor knelt in the private room of the Reverend Mother Superior, and poured out her heart to her as she had done almost two years before. The nun listened wistfully and sadly and stroked the girl's pale-gold hair. It had been one of her most cherished wishes that Eleanor should join the little band of Sisters in the convent, but now it was being doomed out of the girl's own mouth as she knelt at her knee.

'I want him so much, Mother,' she whispered breathlessly. 'Oh, there must be glory, and no shame in saying it . . . I want him!'

The Reverend Mother smiled with tears suspiciously near her eyes. It has ever been the way of youth, to take what it wants. And certainly love and life seemed full of promise for Eleanor Appleby now. The Reverend Mother asked, who was she to hold them apart?

Thus in the silent watches of the night it was settled that Eleanor Appleby should leave the convent almost at once and marry Alec Portal.

He was waiting for her outside the convent gates with the early morning sunshine, as he had said. An hour he waited, growing ever more impatient with a lover's eagerness, whilst the dew on flower and fern all round became transformed into the rising mist that gives promise of a glorious day.

At last she came down the garden path, all in delicious white, with the Mother Superior at her side.

His heart thumped painfully at the sight of her.

He wanted to take this child-woman and lift her high in the sunlight, to look at her, and then to lower her in his arms, until the warm little face and the intoxicating lips were near his own.

But now she had come near, with the nun sympathetic but grave behind her.

'Alec,' she began breathlessly, 'there were several things we forgot to talk about, to arrange, last night. I—I haven't told you that I have no money, except a tiny bit that my mother left me. I—the other, I deeded to his relatives,' she faltered.

'That's fine,' he said eagerly. 'I have tons, and to spare. You must come with me, and at once.'

'Oh, I can't,' she faltered. 'It—there must be arrangements. I—it is all so quick.'

'I have arranged everything,' he said with a lover's masterfulness. 'I have wired to my mother, dear, and she will arrive in Paris this evening, to care for you—until we can be married. I am arranging for a special licence, and then—my dear, our honeymoon at last!'

What could she do, or say, to deter this whirlwind lover? She had a hint of the ruthless masterfulness of him now, and secretly she adored it. The Mother Superior smiled and shook her head, but Alec was not to be gainsaid. It lived with Eleanor ever afterwards, that eager hot-headed discussion of their plans. Alec was like a spoilt boy who must have his way; and have his way he did in the end. It was arranged that he should call for Eleanor late that afternoon and take her to Paris, where his mother would be waiting to meet them.

And when the sun was laying its drugget of crimson from sky rim to rim, he came in a big Lagonda car, profusely decorated with flowers, as if, indeed, it were designed for their wedding journey. Alec alighted, looking like a big, overgrown boy, and the gates of the convent opened to usher out Eleanor with the nun at her side.

The Mother Superior smiled, first at the man, and then at Eleanor, and her eyes shone with the blinding light of a great love. Almost timidly she held out her arms to the girl she had loved as a daughter, and Eleanor bit her white lips, and then with a little anguished cry she went into the Mother Superior's arms for the last time.

The Reverend Mother, Teresa, raised her eyes and seemed to address Alec more than the girl.

'Children, you will be happy?' she said with weak earnestness. 'You will be happy together, won't you? I do hope—it has been my fondest wish always that—'

Her voice trailed off. Eleanor remembered little more of that incident, save that with blurred eyes that saw nothing of the evening's beauty she was helped into the car, and Alec was by her side, driving.

Paradise awaited them.

And paradise it proved to be. The hours, the next few days themselves, passed in an almost unbelievable whirl of happiness. The meeting with Alec's mother, who seemed very happy and contented with her son's choice; the sights and gaiety and luxury of Paris; the restaurants, and the Paris streets with their lights winking and spinning, all dazed the girl so long inured to the monotonous quiet of the convent. The shops yielded her a cascade of beautiful things; for now feverish preparations were being made for their wedding.

It all seemed like a happy dream to Eleanor, from which there must come a rude awakening. Surely never a couple so gloriously happy as they! On her wedding morn, Eleanor awoke to find herself softly repeating his name. The sun streamed through the window of her pink and white bedroom, and seemed to give her its blessing and promise of future happiness.

The wedding of maid to man can be a very beautiful thing. And so it was in the case of Alec and Eleanor Portal. The little Anglican church in the heart of Paris was smothered in flowers and the fruits of the harvest. All the friends of the couple seemed to have flocked to the church to offer their good wishes and smile upon those two who had loved so dearly and been so long parted. Never, it seemed, had the strains of the Wedding March sounded so grand and inspiring as when Alec, tall and smiling and most unbelievably boyish, led his white bride down the aisle.

Sunshine and flowers, youth and happiness! They are the real intoxicants of life. Whirled away in the car after her marriage, Eleanor continued to live in a glorious dream, with only the fear of awakening to mar it. Blue skies, lakes; Rome— the Bay of Naples by moonlight—she drank it all in, her heart singing a wild song of happiness because he was by her side. He was such a tender lover—so good—so noble! Sometimes she was frightened by the bewildering joy of this honeymoon of theirs. It all seemed too good to be true. Could such happiness last?

They spent the last two weeks of it at Mentone, that Mecca of the carefree and gay. At nights they danced together in the hotel ballroom that looked on to the sea, and the fairy lights seemed like living jewels . . . And the people smiled as they watched them, for they were obviously so deeply in love.

They had been at Mentone almost two weeks when Alec first spoke of returning home. It was this that Eleanor dreaded. They had not spoken about it thus far, but then there had been so much for them to say to one another that the mundane things of life—work and reality—had been pushed into the background.

But Eleanor had known that it had to come. In her secret heart she feared and dreaded the return to the scene of the tragedy that had marred her life. She would not let Alec see that, however. She knew that all his work—his life, lay in Royston, and that they must go back.

At Mentone, Alec began to receive letters from England. He was getting in touch again.

He would read them after breakfast as they sat on the terrace of their hotel, that overlooked the wondrous blue sea. Eleanor would see the little pucker gather between her husband's eyes; he would smile, and then frown; many times he shot a sharp look over towards her, but Eleanor, with heart beating fast for some unaccountable reason, was constrained to keep her eyes downcast, unable to meet his gaze.

But she knew of what he was thinking. Work—his patients. She told herself that she was wicked not to want to go with him, to be by his side; yet she dreaded the village gossip; she dreaded the thought of the big house that bore the red lamp of Doctor Alec Portal. It was stiff and ugly, and it was right in the heart of Royston . . .

She glanced across scaredly at Alec. He was smiling as he

read a letter he had just opened—for it was after the breakfast hour. The tiny dimples in his cheeks contrasted oddly with the resolute chin of the man. He looked remarkably fit and well and handsome in the flannel trousers and old school blazer that he wore, and she felt a great pride and love welling in her heart.

Suddenly Alec took his pipe from between his teeth and leant towards her, smiling.

'Eleanor . . . little thing,' he said softly, 'don't you imagine that I haven't been reading your thoughts. You dread going home, eh?'

She started, and flushed gloriously as brown eyes looked troubled and frightened at him for a moment.

He put a hand gently on her rounded white arm. 'I've hated to mention it too,' he said. 'But listen, dear; come and see Honeymoon House, where you and I are going to live, all by ourselves. The most secluded and charming old house in Royston, with beautiful grounds; no neighbours. Yes, and by Jove, I'm getting a new car, Eleanor—'

He was all boyish eagerness. Eleanor looked up in flushed surprise. She had known Alec Portal as a country doctor with a more or less flourishing practice; she knew nothing, as yet, of the notice and attention that had been directed on him in medical circles during the last two years, of the influential patients he had gained, and of the general increase in the size of his practice.

Indeed, vaguely Eleanor had wondered how they could afford this honeymoon. Yet she had not dared to shatter their happiness by questioning him about material things.

And now he spoke of a house—the most charming house in Royston—and a car . . .!

He leant a little nearer to her. 'I've taken Capel Manor, darling, on a long lease,' he said softly. 'I thought it would be a surprise for you—our new home. Say you like it, dear; you like the idea of it. I'm having it redecorated and refurnished, and they say that it's nearly finished now, so I want you to come and see it.'

She looked at him, troubled and frightened, yet smiling faintly.

'Alec ... oh ... but what has become of Derek?' she asked breathlessly.

His smile faded and he became grave. 'Poor old Derek Capel,' he said. 'I wonder when he'll ever settle down. Indeed, I wonder whether he'll ever come back to Royston at all, Eleanor. He seemed pretty cut up about—'

He hesitated, and stopped. It was extremely difficult for them to talk about the past as yet. It was queer—awkward, too—but whenever one of them tried to broach the subject that old barrier, intangible, yet stern and forbidding, seemed to rise between them and make them as if strangers.

So they had tacitly avoided mention of anything that had happened—until now. Now Eleanor looked long at Alec, her breath coming a little fast, her glorious brown eyes holding a strange light.

'You say—Derek Capel has left Royston?' she asked in a voice that held vast relief.

'Yes, rather,' he said, puffing at his pipe, and gazing out to sea abstractedly. 'Derek pulled his stakes and went on one of his big game-hunting expeditions just after—you know. I've had three or four letters saying he's having a good time—and he's been wanting to lease the manor, so I took it on. And that's all,' he ended, rather abruptly, turning to her again. 'You know, Eleanor, sometimes I think dear old Derek too, was too dashed fond of you.'

She trembled a little, and her eyes looked very troubled. 'He was,' she said very faintly, and Alec stretched out his hand and placed it over hers.

'We'll forget all that,' he said softly. 'Tell me, dear, do you like my surprise? Will you come with me—tomorrow? I must go home, darling—and see it all. It will be great fun. Think of it. Our new home.'

She looked at him with shining eyes, wholly happy now, wholly glad, and in that moment she seemed to see the man the most beautiful thing that could ever have been created.

'Alec,' she whispered, 'you are too good to me. Oh, my clear, we are going to be so happy . . . so happy!'

He rose from his chair and came round to her side. And while she held his hand at her beating heart, and he kissed her again and again, Eleanor really believed it for the first time. Her dream was all come true. She was married to Alec, and they were going back to Royston to live as man and wife.

And Derek Capel! He was far away.

She had nothing now to fear; the last shadow had fled. Only before her stretched the rose-tinted future.

So thought Eleanor as she made preparation to terminate their honeymoon, and to return to England with Alec. She was happy as she packed trunks and bags, gloriously happy on the boat—

Could she have seen into the little old-world village of Royston the night before their return—could she have seen the strange visitor to the village and marked his mysterious actions, she would not have been so radiantly happy. Rather she would have been struck with fear and terror.

For Mr Quinny had come to the village.

CHAPTER IX

MR QUINNY was a character. His landlady pronounced this judgment upon him the same night that he came to the village, from nowhere apparently, and appeared at the door of her cottage knocking gently but insistently.

She came down the stairs, and opened the door slightly, to see by the light of the candle she held a man with bent back, lips that twitched, and eyes that, behind the pince-nez he wore, had a fixed and curious look.

Mrs Brown, the landlady, was inclined to be frightened at first, though the hour was not late when Mr Quinny called. Indeed, it would be absurd to say that she was frightened of him, or thought that he was potential for harm; for Mrs Brown was a host in herself. She was a formidable woman; but like many such, it was only necessary to scratch her to find a very tender heart.

Mr Quinny's appearance disturbed the motherly old soul. To quote her own words 'he looked shocking.'

His face was yellow, and as he raised his hat he revealed untidily matted hair, heavily streaked with white. He appeared to be a mass of nerves, and his face, that in birthright had been of fine bold sculpturing, was now terribly ravaged. Enfeebled eyes looked intently up at the landlady behind the spectacles he wore, and his mouth twitched—to quote Mrs Brown again— shockingly.

Yet his voice was pleasant and musical; it was the only part of him that seemed to have survived the blast of the storm that had struck him and prematurely aged him.

'Good-evening, madam; I am a weary traveller seeking rest and refreshment,' he began; and Mrs Brown melted to the cultured, wistful tones. 'I saw the honeysuckle at your gate, and

I—ah, yes; may I come in?' He put his stick inside the doorway, and gently insinuated his own person into Mrs Brown's house. He looked about him with a vast relief that seemed pathetic to Mrs Brown somehow.

'I saw the honeysuckle at the gate, and the garden all a-riot with flowers, and I could not resist stopping to have a look,' her caller went on. 'It is such a typically beautiful English country cottage. Then I saw your notice, "Apartments to Let", madam, and then—well, here I am.'

This was not tentative, yet curiously enough Mrs Brown also waived the formalities. She accepted her new lodger in the same spirit of the inevitable as he had apparently come to her.

So the white-haired, kindly old lady took him in, and straightway she began to feel quite interested in her new lodger, not to say sympathetic. In her chintz-covered parlour he sat down wearily, and fumbled with hat and stick in a way that smote her heart. His pleasant, cultured voice acted very largely as a relief from his appearance, and as though he were conscious of this he used it in small talk concerning the charm of the summer evening and the beauty of the countryside.

Mrs Brown was never really embarrassed, however, until he came to the question of her terms. She judged him shrewdly, and in her own lights, he was 'a gentleman come down in the world.'

'Thirty bob,' she said recklessly; 'that's what I usually charge to gentlemen. And that includes three good meals a day, and all conveniences,' she added with an impetuosity that was utterly alien to her. She had been a landlady long enough to calculate that such terms, if kept to the letter, allowed small margin of profit.

He raised his eyebrows and, nervously, with hands that trembled, produced a note-case from his inner pocket.

'Thirty bob! Ah, let me see. The term is synonymous with shillings, is it not? But you really must accept more than thirty shillings a week, madam. Say three pounds. See; take this note-case. It is fairly well stocked. I am so absentminded that I should be obliged if you would mind it for me, and take the money whenever you need it. Otherwise I shall be forgetting to pay you.'

The case was, indeed, well stocked with bank notes and Treasury notes, and, with confidence thus completely established, Mrs Brown began to think in rather a tender way about the honey-suckle round her gate.

The question of an evening meal arose. In a pleasant flurry Mrs Brown cooked her guest steak rissoles and onions, and when he had eaten it he paid her a compliment on her cooking which was by no means undeserved.

As she was clearing away, she paused at the door with the empty plates in her hands, and a faint flush suffused her worn cheeks. When you got used to him, he was a kindly-looking man. It was illness that made him look so bad. He was shaking now though he was sitting near to the fire and the evening was warm. And that continual twitch of the mouth—it was disquieting.

'You want to take care of yourself more, sir,' his landlady said pointedly but kindly. 'A little rest and nourishment should make the world of difference; and you'll get it here.' Then fearing that she had been too bold, she added timidly: 'And what name might I be calling you, please, sir?'

He looked up with a start. Just then his face had appeared very yellow, and full of a taint—the taint that a hot climate and its fevers bring to a man. Trembling violently, and with mouth twitching, he peered through his spectacles at Mrs Brown.

'What's that? Oh, my name. Call me Mr Quinny,' he said, and for a few moments relapsed into apathy.

But he roused from his reverie after a time and, putting on his hat, announced his intention of going for a stroll before retiring. Mrs Brown, watching him from her window, saw her lodger leaning upon his stick and walking slowly as though he relied much upon its aid.

He did not go far, however. She saw him vanish through the doors of the village inn only a few yards from the cottage. And she waited long, but in vain, for his reappearance.

More in sorrow than in anger, she recognised the fact that it was rather the proximity of her cottage to the inn than the clusters of honeysuckle round her gate that had been the magnet to attract her new lodger to her door. The good lady retired at length somewhat pensively to her cosy kitchen. She did not violently disassociate herself with the use of alcohol; in fact she 'used the house herself.' But she began to perceive that her new lodger might be rather a problem.

Within the village inn, Mr Quinny was astonishing the locals. He ordered brandy by the half-tumblerful, and gulped it with a haste that showed urgency and need. His second and third order, however, left him a more composed man, and his hand round the glass lingered on the counter more, though he continued to stare at the ground as if mesmerised by some minute object thereon, and his mouth twitched painfully.

Before it was necessary to turn all customers out, however, Mr Quinny straightened himself and left the inn very erectly and without the aid of his stick. The potent spirits had performed a temporary miracle in him. The gaping yokels saw that his figure was almost soldierly, and there was something about the slope of his shoulders, the carriage of his head, that in both horse and man speaks of the thoroughbred.

Mr Quinny did not go straight back to his lodgings. He started on a walk, and the pale quarter moon, it seemed, fell over on its back and laughed and mocked at him. For Mr Quinny wilted. The revivifying effect of his potations passed. He looked round him, and the night seemed full of whispers to him; and he was once more a haggard, bespectacled old man, trembling with ague, and in the grip of that virulent giant, John Barleycorn.

He had recourse to a small, flat bottle which he dragged awkwardly from his hip pocket. Again it had its magical effect; or, at least, it sustained the queer dignity that the man had assumed. He had paused on the narrow footpath opposite the lodge gates of what appeared to be a large mansion, and now he plunged across the road, quickly, with stumbling steps, and passed through the gates, walking up a winding carriage drive.

Lights were twinkling from the house when at last Mr Quinny came within sight of it. He paused and adjusted his pince-nez, and his face was working convulsively as he stared at the rambling, low-built old Tudor mansion.

Suddenly a shadow loomed across the gravel path. It resolved itself into the figure of a man whose elephantine frame and grizzled, sombre face were lit by the glow of the pipe he was smoking. Scotland Yard knew that figure of Chief Inspector Brent well. Mr Quinny stood still as a statue at his approach, and so they came to confront one another.

The eyes of the big man were speculative as they rested on the rigid figure of Mr Quinny. A pale amber light from one of the windows of the house fell on Mr Quinny, and showed that his very poise proclaimed indignation. He was staring at the big man intently, suspiciously, through his spectacles.

'Good-evening, sir,' the big man boomed, deeming courtesy in its ordinary phrases at least due to this curious intruder.

'Good-evening to you,' Mr Quinny rejoined sharply. 'I suppose you are here for the same purpose as I am. You are watching this house.'

Chief Inspector Brent of Scotland Yard grimaced.

'To tell you the truth,' the Yard man said in an unwonted burst of confidence, 'a strange fancy brought me here tonight. I can hardly account for it myself. I am like the hound that sniffs at the old and disused lair of the fox. I came here with the feeling that something untoward hung over the house. A feeling that something was going to happen.'

Mr Quinny suddenly laughed—and it was satanic, jeering laughter. It was flung to the trees that girded them all around, and it seemed to die in a shocked echo.

'Inspector Brent,' Mr Quinny said, pronouncing the name

with distinctness; 'you are a fool. You are still trying to solve
the riddle of Professor Appleby's death. Or shall we say his
murder? You will never do that, though it may be solved for
you. I myself am trying to puzzle out the reason for it all—why
he died in the manner he did.'

Inspector Brent started forward a pace. The fact that he was
recognised was overwhelmed by a greater surprise.

'You know something?' he exclaimed, with an ominous
harshness in his voice. And under his penetrative stare Mr
Quinny's mouth twitched, and fear shone luminously in the
eyes behind his spectacles. But in a moment he jerked himself
erect, protected again by that strange dignity that cloaked his
grotesqueness.

'I do know something,' he said quietly. 'I have yet to learn
why Professor Appleby died. It is a matter that has puzzled me
these last two years. But if, and when, that question is satisfac-
torily answered, I shall unmask his murderer and see that justice
is done. Good-night to you, sir.'

He was turning away, but Inspector Brent detained him.

'May I ask who are you, sir?'

'You may call me a detective if you like,' Mr Quinny said
coldly. He peered up at the other. 'At least I have as much right
in the grounds of Capel Manor as you, inspector. I should
imagine that the case of Professor Appleby has lapsed and the
files have been long neglected at Scotland Yard. It was one of
your failures, eh?'

The sneer was so palpable that the detective winced; and a
hot retort hung fire on his lips. But he dissembled his wrath
and like the old fox he was, his words came cunningly.

'I have some right here, sir,' he said truthfully enough. 'Doctor
Portal, who is the new tenant of Capel Manor, did me the
honour to write me asking me to make many of the arrangements
for his homecoming with his wife. I, as a matter of fact, begged
him to let me do so. Why I talk to you so frankly as this I don't
know . . .' he broke off.

'You have been trying to make amends for the prosecution f—his wife?' said Mr Quinny with a new softening.

'That's it, sir,' said the grizzled old inspector gruffly. 'It may)und a queer anomaly, but I'm their friend now. I was chiefly istrumental in bringing them together in the end. In fact,' he ided with some pride, 'I am to be one of the guests at the)usewarming tomorrow when Alec Portal brings home his ride.'

Mr Quinny's mouth twitched, then he threw up his head.

'For the matter of that I am to be a guest also,' he said in a ueer voice. 'That is, if I can see my way clear to come. In hich event I shall have the pleasure of seeing you again, ispector Brent. For the present I will wish you good-evening.'

He turned and stumbled a little uncertainly down the carriage rive towards the gates, leaving Chief Inspector Brent of cotland Yard gnawing his moustache and cursing himself for lking so freely. It was utterly unlike him. He was a taciturn ian whose reticence was a by-word. But tonight a queer mood ripped him, and so oppressed him that he was glad to talk to most anyone.

He fell to wondering who the mysterious stranger might be. was a matter on which he was determined to become enlight- ied before long. It worried him. Chief Inspector Brent was)ath to admit of new complications in the case he had studied) arduously.

For his part Mr Quinny made his stumbling way back to is lodgings with a mind that seethed. At times he broke into iraged muttering, and the sum of it was a searing malediction n Chief Inspector Brent for his interference that night. Mr)uinny had gone to Capel Manor with a definite purpose in is mind. In the house was something he wanted, of which he ad been determined to obtain possession, even if he were irced to turn housebreaker to that end. The presence of Chief ispector Brent in the grounds had definitely circumvented is object.

Mr Quinny, indeed, began to realise that the fates wer
playing too bold a part in this affair for him to direct them
And Inspector Brent was an unconscious instrument in the
workings. It seemed that Mr Quinny was given second sight i
this matter, and he knew that events were marching towards
swift denouement.

He was a very tired and enfeebled man when at length h
reached his lodgings and fumbled with the latchkey. Mrs Brow
listening intently, heard him walk quietly enough upstairs t
his room. The light in the landing he turned off, but a ligh
glimmered under his door for quite half an hour.

At length Mr Quinny considered himself sufficiently fortifie
for bed, and he closed his suit-case and turned off the ligh
But he lay awake and trembling in bed. He was full of quinin
and fever. For long hours he controlled himself, and it was afte
his landlady had dropped off into deep slumber that h
commenced to babble.

A very uneasy and troubled night Mr Quinny passed in h
new lodgings. A doctor would have pronounced him a ver
sick man, and the fact became borne upon Mr Quinny himsel
But he fought hard and he had an object in life, a big objec
and it had to be achieved within the next twenty-four hours.

The unmasking of the murderer of Professor Appleby!

So he wrestled with his demons during the long night. H
combated the delirium that was overcoming him step by ste
and if he babbled it was in the low tones of one who has foug
such bouts before. The whole of his life passed in phantasm;
goria before him, and he chuckled sometimes and muttere
insanely. It was only when he lived again the later periods th
horror came to him. He could have shrieked then, and h
clutched in vain at his reeling senses.

The first streaks of the summer dawn found him with th
fever at its height. He was sitting up, leaning over the bed an
gripping the sides of it, staring at the floor . . .

He seemed to see himself lying once more on the banks

he steamy, greasy river, with the dark, tangled hot forest on either side. Once more he was shaking his skinny, yellow fist at that sluggishly flowing river in which lurked the sly crocodile and the weird hippopotamus. All around him lay the hot quiet of equatorial Africa—that maddening quiet that wears and frays a man's nerves to shreds. The taint of Africa was in him—had hold of him—gripped him remorselessly. And he whom it had conquered shook his puny fist and defied it for the last time.

'Curse this country!' he shouted. 'Curse it—curse it! River and tree—man and beast.'

After that outburst he lay back, gasping, realising that he was in a lavender-scented bed amidst sweet English countryside, with the rosy glow of dawn peeping through his window. The passion gradually left him; and in the full blow of the summer morn he rose, looking very yellow and weak, and endeavoured, tumblingly, to dress himself.

He came down to greet the aroma of bacon and eggs which his landlady was cooking, looking more or less calm. In the fever swamps of Africa Mr Quinny would not have cared to wash the perspiration from his face, or to exert himself in any way after such a bout. But he showed in clumsy attempts to help Mrs Brown, and in efforts at conversation, that he really was pathetically grateful to her for the bond of sympathy which she held out to him.

Mrs Brown stood with arms akimbo, watching him as he toyed with his breakfast.

'They do say that Doctor Alec Portal and his bride are coming home this morning,' she said, not so much by way of making conversation as because she was bursting with the news.

He looked up suddenly, and his eyes held their fever glitter for a moment. 'Ah, yes,' he said very gravely.

'You remember her, of course,' Mrs Brown went on with a rush. 'Her as used to be Professor Appleby's wife. A rare scandal there was over his death, and all; and that pore, beautiful girl went through the mill properly. Not that I believe she did it

meself. That Professor Appleby was a strange man be al
accounts—the kind to swallow arsenic on the slightest pretext,
she added, as if he had been a performing animal in a circus.

'Ah, yes,' repeated Mr Quinny. 'I understand that the folk o
the village are giving the happy pair a royal welcome home.'

'That we are,' said Mrs Brown energetically. 'There's bunting
and flags flying from the school-house, and we shall all turn
out to give them a cheer. We're not the kind to turn against our
own folk down here, Mr Quinn, and Doctor Portal is very well
liked and respected in the neighbourhood. As for that pore
sweet girl—'

So she rambled on, and Mr Quinny listened to it all with
grave attention. Her description of the housewarming and enter
tainments that were to take place at Capel Manor that night
were particularly vivid. Apparently all the gentlefolk of the
countryside, and many of Doctor Portal's important London
patients had accepted invitations. Mr Quinny smiled once in a
wry fashion at his own thoughts.

'I must go and see this village welcome,' he decided aloud
at length. And at about half-past eleven in the morning his
landlady had the gratification of seeing him walking out, fairly
erect and in a well-cut if worn suit, past the tempting doors o
the village inn, and on towards the railway station. Mrs Brown
congratulated herself that she was diverting her lodger's mind
from whatever troubles obsessed him.

The heat of the morning was relieved by a pleasant breeze
that danced down from the hills, and the gay bunting and flags
were all merrily astir in the High Street when Mr Quinny
reached it. The little village of Royston seemed to be given over
to holiday, for the High Street was lined on either side with
people in their Sunday best, waiting for the happy bride and
bridegroom. It was in effect a spontaneous gesture of affection
and loyalty to the doctor who had worked so long and hard in
their midst, and his bride, whose sad story everybody knew.

Mr Quinny took up a position at the end of the street beyond the range of chatter and gaiety. He was shaking in every limb once more, and his mouth was twitching convulsively. This cursed fever never left him for long nowadays.

But he had not long to wait. Soon the car containing Alec and Eleanor came slowly along the High Street, as if, indeed, it were a royal procession. Eleanor Portal, almost breathlessly beautiful all in white, and looking gloriously happy, smiled delightedly with brown eyes shining on all who welcomed her. Alec by her side looked very proud of his wonderful bride, and pleased and handsome, if a little self-conscious. It was unanimously decided that they made a splendid young couple.

Mr Quinny adjusted his pince-nez with a shaking hand as the car came within range of him. Then he swallowed convulsively, and peered forward. The sun's rays fell aslant his face as he did so, and dealt with him unmercifully—just as Eleanor, looking smilingly through the windows of the saloon car, met his gaze.

The metamorphosis in Eleanor was instant and complete. The colour fled from her face, leaving her ghostly, and her glorious eyes dilated. Subconsciously she pulled at Alec's sleeve, her heart beating as if to stifle her.

'Look!' she gasped. 'Alec . . . oh! . . . look . . . That man!'

Her husband turned instantly, and saw a man with matted, overgrown hair, a face yellow and ravaged and indescribably sombre, peering at them through black-rimmed pince-nez. That was all. He appeared to be carelessly dressed in clothes that had once been good; his necktie was awry with his collar, and his jacket was crumpled; his trousers had no semblance of a crease, and it might be that his finger-nails were black. But there were many such men in the world, men who had thrown appearances to the winds. What was there about this man to cause Eleanor such extreme terror?

Then Alec Portal saw the sudden twitch of Mr Quinny's lips, and being a doctor he recognised all the symptoms.

'Poor fellow,' he said softly. 'He's a human derelict. One of life's wrecks.' He laid his capable hand on his wife's slender, trembling one. 'Darling, what's wrong?' he added with new concern. 'You look as white as a sheet.'

'Don't you recognise him?' she whispered. 'I—I'm sure I know him. I've seen him before . . . And he looks so terrible.'

'Pooh,' her husband laughed, gently scoffing as a man will to allay a woman's fears. 'You're getting nervy already, dear. Every one you see is a ghost. You mustn't go on like that, otherwise I shall have you as a patient on my hands very quickly.'

Still she did not smile.

'I think,' she said slowly and with difficulty, 'it is George, the old gardener. He has changed a lot. You know George who used to be with—with the professor.'

Alec threw back his head and laughed.

'George!' he exclaimed, slapping his knee. 'Why, he's the chief gardener at Lady Vawdry's. Eminently respectable, and a total abstainer. A churchwarden, too, dear, and a most impressive figure in his Sunday black. I'm afraid he'd snort with indignation if he heard that poor fellow identified as himself.'

Eleanor's colour was coming back, and she breathed more easily. It must be as Alec said. She was foolishly allowing herself to become a prey to all sorts of absurd fears. It was not brave, nor was it fair to him.

She had sworn to herself that she would be to Alec a perfect wife, never consciously failing him in the slightest detail. She loved him so much, and she knew that, as yet, he adored her. It gave her an awful thrill of fear to think that she might do something to kill that love. If that happened she believed it would be best for her to die.

So she tried to smile, and to banish her fear—yet it persisted at the back of her mind. She would not try to capture elusive memory, yet she was more than vaguely troubled, and a little abstracted during the rest of the drive. She knew that somewhere she had seen that man before; she had known him—he had played some part in her past life. But what? Who was he?

Alec was very tender with her. He felt that, of necessity, she must feel some strain on returning home again. But with the goodwill and affection of everybody, he hoped—nay believed— that she would learn to forget the past and live only for the happiness that life held for her.

And then there was the house. Their new home! As they came in sight of it, its long drive of stately elms, its newly painted lodge and its trim lawns glinting green in the shimmering sunshine, her husband leant towards her.

'Old Derek wrote to say that he hoped we would be very happy at Capel Manor,' he said softly. 'He was a good sportsman—a white man for all his faults.'

She nodded, her eyes suspiciously moist. 'Poor, dear Derek,' she whispered, as if it were a prayer. 'I hope he is safe and happy, Alec.'

He squeezed her hand. It was his own wish, too, for he felt the victor's concern and regard for a vanquished and chivalrous rival. Often of late he had thought of the absent wanderer and wished him well, for it is a mean man who will wish the gods to grin on himself alone.

Now the car had drawn up outside the front door of Capel Manor, and Eleanor and Alec alighted. A small retinue of servants stood on the front steps to greet them, and Eleanor, covered in blushes and confusion, could only nod shyly at their expressions of greeting and welcome.

A thought came back to her, a memory of Professor Appleby giving orders to the terrified servants in his thin, metallic voice, treating her, his wife, as one of them. For an instant she envisioned him, standing with his back to the fireplace in that sumptuously furnished study of his, his eyes aglitter behind his monocle, as he listened through the microphones to all that went on in that house—that house entangled in the snarl of suspicion!

But she banished the terrifying memory. It caused her to feel weak, trembling.

She was with Alec now, and, like children hand in hand on a voyage of discovery, they were wandering round their new home. She exclaimed with delight at everything she saw. Everything was wonderful. The kitchen was a miracle of household economics and modern improvements. Here she was to reign as queen. The rooms, with their broad bay windows looking on to sunlit lawns, were tastefully and expensively furnished. The bedroom was a bedroom such as a woman dreams about but seldom attains, and a white bathroom mutely preened itself on being the acme of immaculateness.

Eleanor began to wonder whether the husband she had married was a fairy prince or a millionaire.

'Alec,' she said in a hushed tone, almost shocked; 'you must have spent an awful lot of money. But, you dear, dear boy, it's simply wonderful—like a fairy palace.'

Doctor Alec Portal did look absurdly like a big overgrown boy. As she smiled at him, and he smiled back at her, she decided that she adored the tiny dimples in his firm cheeks. They detracted from his hawk-like appearance. He was so tall and strong, and she knew that he could look so strong that—yes, she liked the dimples.

And he? Well, he looked at her, and to save himself from incoherent babbling, he drew her to him and placed an arm round her slim shoulders. Sometimes the sight of her dazzling loveliness was almost too much for him.

'Come, darling; there's one place you haven't seen, and that's my consulting room. It used to be Derek's study, and I've kept it as it was because the old fellow sent me a telegram right at the last moment asking me not to make any alterations in the furnishing. A little queer of him, eh? But I suppose it's some sentiment, so of course I've respected it. Come and see where the money spider is going to weave his web, darling.'

Laughingly she went with him. She protested that it was a shame that everything should be new except his consulting room. But when they entered Derek Capel's study there seemed little to complain about. The luxury-loving owner of Capel Manor had exquisite taste. A great thick pile carpet covered the wide expanse of the room; there were rugs everywhere, and deep arm-chairs; an extremely handsome bookcase lined one side of the wall, and above the wide fireplace was an elaborate overmantel holding two photographs in silver frames.

As if attracted magnetically towards them both, Eleanor and her husband crossed towards the fireplace.

Doctor Alec Portal took up one of the photographs. It was of Derek himself, and it had been facing one of Eleanor. Derek, handsome and smiling, with his glossy hair brushed back and that latent recklessness lurking in the romantic, dark-fringed eyes. Alec held it out to the woman he loved, and they looked queerly at one another, as if the same thought had passed through the minds of both.

How had Derek Capel used his life since he had vanished? Irresponsible, unstable as water, and too finely tempered, he was the type of man to take a blow badly. On the other hand, he had great gifts which he might have used wisely and for the betterment of the world. These two who were so splendidly happy felt vaguely troubled as they stared at this photograph of him in the full flush of his manhood.

'Poor Derek,' Eleanor said wistfully. 'Oh, I do hope he has fallen in love with some nice girl and married her.'

Alec replaced the photograph, and tried to turn her thoughts into more cheerful channels.

'How am I ever going to settle down to stern duty amidst all this splendour?' he asked in mock despair. 'And I'm afraid you'll have to take that photograph of yourself away, darling, otherwise I shall spend all my time looking at it, and that'll mean worse heart trouble than I have already.'

She laughed like a little child, and taking up a pair of his medical stethescopes that were lying near, beckoned to him.

'Come here, Alec,' she commanded. 'Let me test that heart of yours. I don't really believe you've got one.'

With the 'phones over her ears she listened.

'Isn't it thumping madly?' he asked at length, longing to take her in his arms.

'Too much smoking, sir,' she pronounced demurely, and the next moment he took a kiss from her as penalty.

Time was forgotten by them during the next half hour as Eleanor helped him to arrange his medical books. When they remembered that they were to entertain guests that night at their housewarming they agreed together that it was a nuisance, and that they would much rather have been alone.

'We shall have to hurry though. Alec,' she said, suddenly brisk. 'See. I'll place these instruments in the drawers of your desk for the time being, so that you'll know where to find them when you want them.'

She pulled out one or two of the drawers, and hastily crammed his things into them. It was when she grasped the handle of the topmost right-hand drawer that she met with a rebuff. The drawer would not open.

She tugged, but it would not yield.

And suddenly a queer, inexplicable fear struck at her heart. 'Alec,' she called before she had time to think. 'There's something wrong here. The drawer won't open.'

He crossed to her side swiftly, and tried it.

'No,' he said with a shake of his head after a moment; 'it won't open, darling. Derek must have locked it.'

Then, indeed, every instinct reared up all at once and warned Eleanor. Her brain performed swift, acute evolutions, like some finely constructed and perfectly timed piece of mechanism. Derek had locked this drawer. Why?

All in a moment her breath was coming swiftly, and the lovely colour had fled from her face leaving her perfectly white. She bent over the desk to hide her emotion from Alec.

That letter! All in a flash she remembered the damning letter she had sent to Derek Capel on the night of Professor Appleby's death. At night she had implored him to come over o her aid, knowing that Professor Appleby was in one of his most devilish humours, and in desperate rebellion against her fate she had added to her letter those awful words; 'He is not fit to live. If I had the courage I believe I would kill him myself.'

Now she understood. That was why Derek had wired at the last moment to ask that his study should be left unmolested. He had locked that accusing letter in this drawer, and he had remembered it when it was too late.

Treacherous, miserable Fate that seemed to dog Eleanor Portal all through fear and unhappiness. She was free—free for all her life! Doomed to time from the far-reaching hand of the Law. But that which she valued far above life itself—her husband's love—was now at stake. She knew, just as certainly as she knew that the letter was in this drawer, that if Alec discovered it and read it his faith in her would be shattered, and no protestations, no proof of innocence or affection or loyalty on her part could ever rebuild it.

All these thoughts passed in a whirl through her brain as she tugged ineffectually at the drawer.

She must get rid of Alec—get him out of the room, if only for a few minutes, while she recovered that letter. She was trembling, nearly swooning. She must not let him see her like this. Oh, God, if he saw that letter it would mean the end of all things for her.

'Can't you get it open, dear—try hard.' His pleasant voice maddened her.

She kept her head bent and tugged again at the drawer. It seemed to her for an awful moment that the lock was going to yield. Heavens! it must not do that while he was there. Her wealth of fair hair had tumbled a little, and she was aware that her breathing was uneven. She could have screamed with the tension and fear of that moment.

Agitation had her completely in its grip, and she was convicting herself by her own demeanour. Alec was looking at her curiously, and with growing concern. Somehow she must get rid of him—she must.

She remembered all at once the bunch of keys which the housekeeper had handed to her. It provided a way out.

'Alec,' she gasped. 'Go up to the bedroom and get the keys. One of them may fit. Please—hurry!'

He stared at her, the concern growing in his eyes. What was all this fuss about a locked drawer? What was the matter with Eleanor, anyhow? He did not fail to notice the agitated rise and fall of her bosom, and he began to grow more alarmed.

'Silly little darling,' he said, trying to take her in his arms. 'What does it matter, anyhow—a locked drawer? One of the servants will find the key and open it. Come, you mustn't upset yourself over these trifles—why, I declare, you're shaking!'

But she shook him off, her white face quite tragic, her eyes shining feverishly.

'Alec . . . oh please,' she said, with almost a moan. 'Go and get the key . . . it's only upstairs . . . just to please me.'

Loverlike he gave in to her. But his own face was uneasy as he went from the room. She heard him going up the stairs with quick steps, and she knew that she had only a little time . . . only a little time!

Frantically she tugged at the recalcitrant drawer now. For so slender a person she seemed endowed with superhuman strength. The whole desk shook, and a little moan broke from her as still the drawer resisted. Her white teeth clenched on her lower lip; she tugged again like one possessed, and at last with a snap, and a sound of splintering wood, the drawer flew open.

Almost sick with apprehension, she rummaged frantically amongst the few papers in the drawer. She pounced on one that was familiar—a folded sheet of notepaper—and opened it. Yes, it was her own letter to Derek Capel. Her eyes followed the few hastily scribbled lines, while her breath came sobbingly. An awful sick fear flooded her soul as the words danced before her, and she realised the full significance that could so easily be placed upon them.

She must destroy this letter—at once.

She was about to crunch it tightly in her hand, to tear it into minute fragments, when a voice, sharp with horror and accusation, fell upon her like a whip-lash.

'Eleanor! My God!'

She whirled round, to see Alec standing there, grim and tight-mouthed, his eyes filled with a dawning horror and loathing. So close they were that they almost touched, but he fell a step back. She cried out like one in pain at that instinctive action, and flung out her hands blindly to him.

'Alec . . . oh, my dear . . . forgive me!'

He had seen. She knew that. He had read the letter over her shoulder. Alarmed, and perhaps made suspicious by her strange agitation, he must have come down the stairs very quietly and almost crept into the room behind her.

'My God, Eleanor, to think that you . . .'

'No, no,' she cried, stung to self-defence by his measured, horrified tone. 'It's not true, Alec, I swear it on my life. Don't think that of me. Alec—oh my dear. I need you now. Hold me . . .'

But he deliberately retreated as her slim, lissom form swayed towards him. His handsome face was distorted, and a great loathing of her was in his face and eyes. To Alec Portal it seemed then that his world had come tumbling in ruins about his head. Very bitterly aloud he breathed the remaining part of his sentence . . .

'To think that—you—are—a murderess!'

She went down on her knees at his feet, great agonised sobs shaking her frame. Her slim white arms wrapped around him, and words came from her quivering lips in little gasps.

'No—no. Alec, you mustn't say that. Have pity—have mercy on me! I was young—younger then—and life seemed Hell to me. I wrote that letter . . .'

She broke down, incapable of speech, great gulping sobs wrenched from her parted lips. Fear, like a red-hot knife, was stabbing in her heart, turning and twisting there. Whatever she said, there remained the incontrovertible fact that she had written that letter.

What view would the jury at her trial have taken of it if they had seen it? How different might their verdict have been!

'Guilty!'

Alec looked down at her with that loathing in his eyes that nearly made her swoon with fright. Thoughts were searing his mind, thoughts of her who crouched at his feet, sobbing as if her heart would break; and they were not nice thoughts for a man to have of a woman. He stared at the wealth of fair hair, the slim white column of her neck, and for a moment he had a mad impulse to crush the life out of it. That lissom, sweet figure, the trimly arched ankles, they were used consciously to lure and cheat men. The Delilah! She had got his name, and his protection. She had cheated him!

Eleanor, shaking like a child that has been whipped, stretched up her arms to him. 'Alec—oh, my dear boy,' she whispered closing her eyes, with tremors passing across her white face, 'if you look at me like that I shall die. Won't you try to believe— won't you? I appeal to you see—'

She tried to rise to him, but he backed away in horror.

'No, no—don't touch me!' he blazed. And then, picking up the letter that had fallen, he crossed to the mantelpiece, leaning on it and burying his head in his hands. While Eleanor stood as if a seismal shock were wreaking destruction all around her Very white, very calm, and very strange she looked as she stood there in the centre of the room. Her lips were moving voicelessly and had Alec looked at her then he might have had a fright.

But he did not look.

The telephone rang suddenly out in the hall. Both started as if the harsh buzz of it were the last trump. Then a trim parlourmaid came into the study.

'If you please, sir,' she said, suddenly scared at his grim face, 'there's an urgent call from Mrs Brown of No. 3 Acacia Cottages. She says that her lodger, Mr Quinny, seems very ill, and would you come at once, please sir.'

Glad of the distraction, Alec buttoned his jacket. He pushed the crumpled letter in one pocket, and pulled down the flaps, as a man will do unconsciously. Then, without a look at his wife, he hurried from the room.

Like a white ghost, Eleanor was at the window to see the last of him as he went off—the dear face and figure she loved so well. Tears would not come now. But inside of her she was breaking up.

CHAPTER X

THERE was no question but that Mr Quinny was ill. He was, indeed, a shuddering travesty of a man. His walk that morning, when he should have rested in bed, and his subsequent imbibitions at the village inn—which the landlord would bear witness had been exorbitant—had precipitated a crisis in the old gentleman.

On returning to his lodgings he had been seized by an attack. Mrs Brown, whose spirit was generally inexhaustible in emergencies of illness, had been appalled. Mr Quinny raved in delirium, and tore at his collar, gasping for air, and when Mrs Brown tried to get him to lie down, he fought with her. His wasted frame had been possessed of the strength of a tiger; his face had been a yellow mask of fury, a sight to make even his landlady quail.

At length she had sent a messenger hastily to the post office to ring up the doctor.

In his room Mr Quinny fought as he had never fought before the running fire that was in every vein of him, consuming him. Despairingly he tossed and turned on his bed, tearing at the bed-clothes, muttering and shrieking. He was trying to retain a last vestige of reason. He must fight through this attack.

By the time Doctor Alec Portal arrived he had almost emerged from it, his spirit indestructible and shining from his eyes like steel that has been forged in the furnace. Very kindly were those peering eyes behind the spectacles as he raised them at Doctor Alec Portal's entrance. The man himself was limp, shuddering, with the perspiration streaming off his yellow face, but he radiated a feeble kind of geniality.

'Ha! Good-afternoon, doctor. My profound apologies for troubling you at a time like this. You should never have come, sir. I understand your own private affairs command you just now, and—'

'Oh, that's all right,' said Alec Portal brusquely. 'Let's have a look at you—gently now.'

'I felicitate you upon a charming and beautiful wife,' gasped Mr Quinny as he was being examined.

Alec glanced at him sharply. The compliment could scarce be termed an impertinence, considering the whole village had turned out to give the newly married couple a reception. Indeed, half an hour ago Alec would have received it in the spirit in which it was given.

Now his blue eyes bored into Mr Quinny's face; grimness pursed his mouth. 'Thank you,' he snapped. 'It is more to the point, however, that you are a very sick man. Why, good heavens alive, I feel sorry for you, sir. You must know the state you're in.'

'I do,' said Mr Quinny softly. 'Wasn't it Wendy in *Peter Pan* who said that to die would be a very great adventure'?'

Alec, standing at the table, looked again at this queer, pleasant-voiced stranger, and commiseration was in his glance.

'You have courage, Mr Quinny,' he said. 'I understand you have been out in the fever swamps of Africa.'

Mr Quinny's mouth twitched, and he shuddered convulsively.

'But you must remember that you have contributed towards your present condition,' Alec said gently, roused to infinite pity at the contemplation of this human wreck. 'You should have treated yourself scientifically, Mr Quinny. Good lord, man, this idea that the whisky bottle is the cure for all ills will kill you if you go on.'

Mr Quinny merely shook his bent head, too apathetic to care, or listen, apparently.

Alec stood at the table, concocting a dose of medicine. But he suddenly paused and looked up, staring into vacancy. All in a moment the young doctor had lost sight of his case. He was back again in the study with Eleanor, going over again those brief moments of drama. His face betrayed his emotions. His forehead glistened with sweat, and one hand clenched and unclenched. An exclamation was forced softly, huskily, from his lips.

'God, to think that she—'

He stopped, controlling himself, and glanced sharply at his patient. Mr Quinny, who had been so apathetic a moment before, was now turned half-way towards him, and was peering at him with a surprisingly shrewd gleam through his spectacles. A moment the queer tableau endured, and Alec, with a hot flush of shame and anger on his face, took a step forward, with the medicine in his hand.

Mr Quinny took it, and slowly drained the black, thick fluid. He looked up.

'You are not happy, doctor?' he said very softly.

Alec started. But after a second his bent brows relaxed. There was something about this human derelict—an innate understanding and sympathy—that seemed to disarm resentment.

'Who is happy in this world?' asked the young doctor shortly. 'We wail with terror when we come into it, and our subsequent experience generally goes to justify this first instinct.'

'A very nasty aphorism,' said Mr Quinny with a grim little chuckle. As that mirthless sound passed his trembling lips, his right foot, encased in a rough, ill-fitting boot, moved out stealthily two yards, perhaps, over the linoleum. Mr Quinny's head was bent apathetically, but his eyes were very keen, and they were fixed on a white piece of paper on the floor.

The sole of Mr Quinny's boot came down on the piece of paper, and he drew his foot in with the piece of paper under it.

It had fallen from Alec Portal's pocket. In the secret agitation that swayed him, he had indulged in a little mannerism peculiar to him in moments of stress; that of thrusting his hands into his jacket pockets, and then drawing them out again and smoothing down the flaps. In the course of this operation the piece of paper had been brushed out of his pocket and fluttered to the floor.

Now it was under the sole of Mr Quinny's right boot, and it became evident he had no intention of giving it up, or mentioning the matter. He sat shuddering and shrunken, and he said:

'You ask who is happy in this world, doctor. Why, I shall be before I die.'

The doctor started at something almost of prophecy in the human derelict's tone. 'You!' he echoed.

'Why not?' said Mr Quinny, staring moodily into space. 'I have lived long enough, been through sufficient misery for my one moment of happiness. I hope I am not to be cheated of it now.'

'What is your idea of the supreme height of happiness?' asked the doctor curiously.

Mr Quinny jerked his head and peered at him.

'To see the love-light shining from the eyes of a woman,' he said simply.

Whereat Doctor Alec Portal bit his lip, and after giving brief but definite instructions that his patient should take certain medicines, he went outside and conferred with Mrs Brown.

The landlady learned that her lodger was very ill, and must be taken strict care of. In particular, it was important that he should not touch alcohol, that he should go to bed and have careful nursing.

And in the hall where he sat in an alcove, Mr Quinny was reaching down steadily, but with laboured breathing, for the piece of paper he had secreted under his foot. He got it in his hand at last, opened it, and peered at it through his spectacles.

A spasm crossed Mr Quinny's face—a spasm of ineffable sorrow.

'It is as I thought,' he said very quietly. 'The time has come, and I must unmask the murderer of Professor Appleby.'

For he held in his hand the letter that Eleanor had written to Derek Capel two and a half years before; the letter in which she begged Derek to come over, saying that if she had the courage she would kill her husband herself.

It was a damning piece of evidence.

CHAPTER XI

Capel Manor was a cairngorm of lights. Outside in the stabling, motor-cars clustered like great slinky animals crouched on the leash; servants in livery and maids in white aprons and caps hurried to and fro; from the house came the strains of a dreamy waltz.

The ballroom was lit like a silvery cave. Chandeliers composed of thousands of pieces of finely cut glass shed down their lights, and the polished flooring winked them back in a flashing pool. Everywhere laughter and gay chatter mingled with the strains of the orchestra; the sombre black and white of the men's figures were like so many sharp silhouettes against the riot of colour made by the women's toilets. Laughing faces and bright eyes, the sauve gleam of pearls, and over it all the subtle, intoxicating waft of scent. The ballroom was like a fairy top, slowly spinning.

A man who had come through the dark shrubberies of the grounds stopped to peer through the french windows at the scene.

He had the air almost of a gaunt wolf who has been ostracised from the pack and must needs roam alone. His movements were furtive, but fear did not govern them. He crept closer, adjusting his spectacles hanging on their black ribbon that gave him, somehow, an air of sombre distinction, and he peered into the room, peered with a grim, haggard and despairing face.

'My God!' he suddenly whispered; and he turned away and stared with bleak eyes into nothingness.

He had just seen Eleanor Portal floating by in the arms of a cavalier who looked extremely pleased with himself.

Such a dazzling picture of sad loveliness! The peering

stranger had caught her off her guard. If his own face had been despairing, hers had been infinitely more so. Cold, cold as marble! And her tragic brown eyes mirrored her thoughts.

The unseen watcher had been able to read and understand them. Understanding came like a tearing pain, a flash of summer lightning; he clenched and unclenched his hands.

Unable to endure the sight of her again, he sought the man now as he peered once more through the windows. And he glimpsed him through the throng, taller than most men there, standing at the curtained threshold to the ballroom, and looking on moodily while he smoked a cigarette.

Alec Portal's eyes were narrowed, his face dominated by jutting chin and those shining slits as his gaze followed his wife almost savagely all the time; and he was consuming his cigarette immoderately, so that its tip glowed as if with menace.

The man outside in the darkness studied him with peering earnestness.

It was more than the guests in the ballroom dared do. There was not one who was Ajax amongst them to defy the quivering fury that radiated from the man. It would scarce be adequate to say that their host cast a cloud on the festivities. He did more than that. He charged the atmosphere with electricity.

Every one was expectant—excited. Laughter trilled out, chatter hummed dynamically. Forced and false was the gaiety, as if the dancers with shifting feet were whirling gunpowder in a heap and waiting recklessly for the fusion.

The music stopped at the end of the dance. There were some fifty guests, who mainly grouped themselves near the banking of flowers and ferns that screened the orchestra, or stood clapping discreetly for the music to continue.

Alec Portal turned his back contemptuously on the scene and strode out into the hall.

A little group of men gathered together and exchanged meaning sentences. They were mainly country gentlemen who hunted and lived hard, and were outright and direct in their methods. Moreover, they really liked Alec Portal, and if anything was wrong with the old fellow and they could help him—

Having decided, they followed in his wake and made for the hall. And Inspector Brent of Scotland Yard was one who was amongst them.

On the face of it theirs was a quite natural proceeding, for the wide Tudor hall was furnished as a lounge or sitting-out apartment, and here drinks were dispensed and the men might smoke their cigars and become bluff, unaffected males as was their natural wont.

As they came into the hall they greeted Alec with a great show of geniality, and he, who had been standing moodily near the fireplace, roused himself to play his part. He was not sorry for the interruption, for his thoughts were bad.

Siphons fizzed, and hearty voices and laughter warmed the place. Alec had perforce to unbend, which he did fairly creditably, for in the company of others a man momentarily loses the sharp perspective of his own affairs.

But the men were not to shake themselves free from the skirts of the womenfolk for long. The curtains parted, and through them there came the sheen of silk, the glisten of white arms and the flash of jewels to startle and confuse Alec as he looked up. He had just had the idea of finding forgetfulness in this strange business of drinking hard and quickly, an experiment he had never so far in his lifetime attempted.

Zephyrs of music came in from the ballroom, but there were still a few more couples who had evidently decided to sit out that dance, and they drifted in and found themselves seats.

The curtains parted, and Eleanor came into the hall with her dancing partner, Captain Firsk. A tall man of the true army type, he looked a splendid animal in evening coat-tails. His teeth were gleaming in a white bar under his trimmed moustache as he smiled at her. He was in the seventh heaven of bliss.

Eleanor had pleaded a violent headache. But Captain Firsk

simply would not believe it. His experience was that such an excuse meant his partner was not averse from sitting out the dance with him.

He was a personable youngster, fresh and lonely from barrack life, and he hardly knew or cared who she was; it was enough for him that she was charming.

Eleanor had expected a deserted hall, and she threw up her arm as if to ward off a blow as Alec Portal half started up, his face grim. The sight of her seemed to act on him as a rag does to a bull.

Like a child that has been severely punished she slowly dropped her arm, and gazed beseechingly at her husband. Very dainty, very ravishing she looked as she stood there in her white frock with its bell-hoop effect and tiny tuckered sleeves. Her hair was like spun gold, and her distress was surely real enough to melt the heart of the most adamant.

Alec drew himself erect, and recognising that she actually was almost at the end of her tether, he came to her rescue. But there was a biting savagery underlying his tone.

'You are still unwell?' he said in inquiry. And then to the company at large: 'It is most unfortunate, but Eleanor has one of her violent headaches. It is advisable that she should retire for a little while. I do hope you will excuse us. I am sorry, but I know how terrible these headaches are.'

There were instant and polite murmurs of regret.

'The only thing for a crushing headache,' said one amiable woman, 'is to lie down and rest. Don't I know it?'

'I—I think I will go,' Eleanor said in a small voice, and there was poignant pain and despair in her sweet face.

'But . . . Oh, I say, you know—' dissented Captain Firsk, following her to the broad staircase. It was a fact about Tommy Firsk, one that his intimates persistently and publicly proclaimed: his brain was an almost complete vacuity.

Alec Portal interposed between. 'My wife is really unwell,' he said coldly and flatly, and when the youngster had retired discomfited, he turned again to the staircase. Eleanor had halted, and their eyes met. Hers were filled with unspeakable anguish and pleading. Plainly they sent him a mute, terrified message—a message he could not, or would not, read. Inspector Brent read it, however, and in his heart there sounded a tocsin call of fear and warning. She was hardly responsible for her actions.

But Alec Portal's eyes were stony. They stared a negative to her wild appeal, for he believed her guilty of breaking that commandment which civilisation holds in most solemn awe.

She had done it . . . somehow she had done that devilish thing. Poison! In his horror he dared not allow his thoughts to dwell on it: how she had done it, with what cunning and preparation.

He turned from her slowly and deliberately; and with a little half-articulate sound of despair, Eleanor went up the staircase.

Colonel Haddington, the local M.F.H., unconsciously relieved the tension. He was utterly oblivious of all save his favourite topic. Hunting! He stood with his feet astraddle, and his hands behind his back, laying down the law.

There was polite, but bored agreement at intervals to his words, while fans tapped impatiently and cigar smoke spiralled fantastically to the ceiling.

Yet the feeling of suspense was instinct amongst that little company. Even the less acute could feel it, and knew that something was going to happen.

And then, quite suddenly, crashing into Colonel Haddington's voice, there came a sharp, imperative knock at the hall door.

The guests looked at one another. Colonel Haddington ceased speaking. His face became redder, and he stroked his white walrus moustache. A reception hall, even if it is in the Tudor style, has its disadvantages if it abuts on the front door and late callers are permitted to interrupt a masterly monologue.

Alec Portal rose quickly, and went to the door himself. Curiously enough he had become calm, momentarily. He had his finger on the pulse of the company, and he knew it had become jumpy, nervy. He regretted his own passionate gestures of the early evening, and saw himself as a swash-buckler of emotions.

His situation called for a frozen calm.

It was just the sordid problem of a wife he did not want. Lawyers and people could arrange for a separation. He'd treat Eleanor generously—

Thinking in this wise he threw open the front door. And his thoughts performed quick gymnastics. For a shadow fell athwart the wall; the shadow of a man, very erect, who wore a soft velour hat and pince-nez spectacles on a black cord.

The staring guests saw only the shadow, and there was something in the sombre orthodoxy of that silhouette that set them on tenterhooks of expectation. But Alec Portal saw Mr Quinn in the flood of light from, the hall, and he had a flash back of memory, quick, elusive, tantalising. It came and it was gone. It left him with the baffling conviction that he had seen this man before some time long ago. But he could not quite remember.

'Good Heavens, man!' he exclaimed sharply; 'what are you doing abroad at this time of night? I told you to go to bed. Why, you're ill—very ill!'

'Something called me here,' came Mr Quinny's voice. 'Voices called. They told me I had some affairs to put in order. It may be that I am ill . . . the fever! But I had to come.'

'You'd better come in,' Alec said quickly.

Mr Quinny came in, shaking, yellow, his eyes the miserable abashed eyes of the human derelict who shuns society. The sight of him came as a shock to the guests, who exclaimed in horror. Mr Quinny had become oblivious of them, however. He was peering through his black-rimmed spectacles at the walls and up the broad staircase to the balcony above, hung with exquisite oil paintings and tapestries, and presently a bitter smile formed on his lips.

The palsied figure brushed past Inspector Brent without

seeing him. The Yard man stood back, very distinguished in his evening clothes, a figure of solid impassivity. But his eyes under their heavy-lidded droop of mastery flickered over the company, and settled always on Mr Quinny. Even Inspector Brent, the self-appointed sentinel, was uneasy.

Amid a tense silence Alec Portal piloted the human wreck to a settee, and seating him, he poured out for him a stiff measure of spirits. This the palsied man accepted with a courteous little inclination of his head, and carrying it shakingly to his lips, he gulped it down.

He seemed to relax into apathy then, staring at the floor with the empty glass in his trembling hand, his mouth twitching convulsively. His yellow, fever-ridden face was in the last stage of emaciation, but he was certainly more cred-itably groomed than on the last occasion Alec had seen him. His linen was clean, and so were his long tapering hands, and a desperate effort had evidently been made to polish his rough boots. His landlady was even then wringing her hands over Mr Quinny, who had departed her cottage almost in a state of collapse, but with some feverish obsession in his brain.

'Ladies and gentlemen,' Alec said quietly, 'Mr Quinny is an unfortunate gentleman who has contracted a hectic fever in Africa. It is now in its remittent stage, and I am sure you will sympathise with him deeply.'

Murmurs of condolence arose. One or two Women got up and left hastily with their escorts, unable to endure the ghastly appearance of Mr Quinny.

It was Colonel Haddington, Master of the Hounds, who, once again, came to the rescue.

'Africa, eh?' he boomed. 'May I inquire, sir, if you had any sport out there? I mean that kind of thing,' and he waved a hand largely towards the trophies that decorated the walls.

'Big game hunting?' said Mr Quinny listlessly, and without looking up. 'Yes; I have done some of it.'

'Aha!' exclaimed Colonel Haddington in derision. 'Nothing like the sport in this country, sir, the joy of the chase, the—'

'By Jove!' interrupted Tommy Firsk, in sudden interest. 'I remember now. The owner of this place used to be a big game hunter. Didn't he quit the country after that murder trial over Professor Appleby? He was in love with the woman, or something. I remember it was quite a sensation. A beautiful woman, by gad I and everybody was glad she got off scot-free.'

A hush fell on the company. It was a long-sustained and painful silence. Never in all his irresponsible career had Tommy Firsk produced such a profound sensation. Metaphorically he had flung a flaming torch to a stream of petrol.

Women fidgeted, and one man coughed. None dared look at Alec, who stood like, a statue, his face gray and creased. But the battery of outraged eyes that was turned on Firsk informed that gentleman that he had committed some terrible *faux pas*.

'I mean to say, you know,' he stammered, plunging in still further, 'it's all jolly interesting. No one ever cleared up the mystery.'

It was then that Mr Quinny spoke. His voice was listless, loaded with lethargy, and his vacant gaze was still fixed on the floor.

'The police blundered badly,' his voice droned. 'The murderer of Professor Appleby should have been unmasked on the night of the crime, and justice done.'

Inspector Brent was suddenly goaded past himself. 'I don't know who you are, sir,' he cut in incisively, 'but you have once before hinted that you could throw light on this matter. I deeply regret that the subject has been brought up, but since it has, I think you should explain yourself more fully.'

Mr Quinny looked up and stared at him across the space that divided them.

'Your words were deliberately meant as an affront to me,' the inspector added angrily. 'Let us hear your solution of the case then. Let us see whether your amateur theories can enlighten professional experience.'

Mr Quinny shook his head slowly. 'Experience is the schoolmaster of fools, inspector,' he said dispiritedly.

'I think I could trace that epigram to another author than yourself, sir,' sneered the inspector bitterly. 'So far you are not original.'

'Why bicker?' Mr Quinny said wearily. 'It is probable that there are many variations of the saying, which goes to prove that it is old and a truism. I blame you, inspector. I blame you deeply for not catching the murderer of Professor Appleby red-handed and fixing the guilt beyond all shadow of doubt. It was so easy for you to have done so.'

Alec Portal sprang forward, his handsome face convulsed. He could no longer stand the strain of the ordeal.

'You can tell me something,' he cried hoarsely, grasping Mr Quinney's shoulders with a strength he did not suspect. 'You can tell me beyond all shadow of doubt who—who murdered Professor Appleby?'

Mr Quinny slowly lifted his livid face, but the peering eyes behind the spectacles went past Alec to the balcony above. There sounded a little gasp up there, and a woman's white gown whisked out of sight. But no one appeared to observe it, save, perhaps, Mr Quinny.

His head sunk again. 'I can name the murderer,' he said listlessly, 'and I can produce complete evidence of his guilt.'

Alec Portal gazed at him in horror and fear, not daring to ask the question that trembled on his lips. And suddenly a spark of vitality animated Mr Quinny. He lifted his head.

'Please sit down, and let me tell the story from the beginning,' he said quietly.

And when Alec had obeyed him he fumbled in his pocket and produced a piece of paper. 'I will be as brief as possible,' he said with a queer huskiness suddenly catching his voice. 'To begin properly, I would remind you of the terrible existence that the unfortunate lady, who is really the subject of this discussion, led with her husband, Professor Appleby. He was a meglomaniac of cruelty. The greatness that had come to him had partially unhinged his brain. He dealt in subtleties. He liked to see things suffer . . . and the chief object of his cruelty was his extremely lovely and innocent young wife.

'Imagine her tortures,' Mr Quinny went on, 'the suffering that gradually brought her to snapping point . . . Well, I think some of you know.

'On the night of the tragedy, Eleanor Appleby, as she was then, was almost overcome by terror. Her husband's cruelty had reached its zenith. It seemed that he had crossed the border line at last, and had become a coldly raging maniac, whose only idea was to hurt her—to bring her to the same state as himself.'

Mr Quinny paused and peered round at the company. No longer was his voice at variance with his hectic flush and glittering eyes, for it had taken on a vibrant tense note.

'In her desperation that night she did a mad thing,' he went on. 'She wrote a letter to another man who loved her, asking for his help. Ah! you didn't know that, Inspector Brent. That letter was never produced at the trial. There it is—read it!' And he feebly tossed the piece of paper he had been holding from his hand so that it fell to the carpet.

Alec with a sharp cry made to procure it, but Inspector Brent was before him, and snatched it up almost from under his hand. A primitive, lawless instinct seemed to have broken loose in the room, for the guests now got to their feet and crowded round him, trying to read it over his shoulder.

The C.I.D. man's face was thunderous as he read that letter. In a hoarse, low voice he repeated aloud the damning phrase Eleanor had written.

'He is not fit to live. If I had the pluck I believe I should kill him myself.'

'This letter should have been produced at the trial,' he said harshly, as he held it up. 'Where did you get it? Who held it back?'

Alec said nothing. He was staring at Mr Quinny as if at a ghost, wondering how he had lost that letter, wondering how it had come into the mysterious stranger's possession.

'Inspector, you will begin to understand why I say you have blundered,' Mr Quinny went on. 'That was one important piece of evidence missed at the trial.'

The Yard man drew a deep breath. 'If this is genuine,' he said slowly and sternly, 'it is certainly very incriminating.'

Mr Quinny, sitting huddled on the settee, suddenly lifted his head. 'Who does it incriminate?' he asked sharply.

The Yard man forgot all judiciousness in his chagrin, for now he, too, thought he had been tricked. 'It incriminates Eleanor Portal,' he returned angrily.

As if he had been struck a blow, Mr Quinny turned his twitching features up to the balcony. Up there he caught a glimpse of her who had been named; he heard a broken cry in a woman's voice, and hurrying footsteps.

'You fool! You fool, Inspector Brent!' he suddenly cried, his whole frame shaking. 'All through this case you have flown a kite without a tail, and allowed it to rush where it will in the winds of prejudice, ignorance and hasty reasoning. Doesn't that letter tell you more than that? Look, man! Look to whom it is addressed.'

A sudden stupefied expression crossed Inspector Brent's face. He stared at the letter again, and his lips voicelessly framed the words:

'Derek Capel!'

'The man who loved her,' said Mr Quinny, his voice suddenly intensely vehement, charged with scorn and loathing, 'The man who posed to himself that he would have died for her! And yet he allowed her to be crucified while he watched with closed lips. He could have told so much at the trial. And yet he kept silent. And afterwards he made good his disappearance from the country. Why?' Mr Quinny leant forward, his yellow face dank, his eyes glittering behind his spectacles. *'Because Derek Capel was the murderer of Professor Appleby!'*

His listeners drew sharp breaths. Though they had half expected it within the last few seconds, they were curiously horrified to hear the broken man utter that blistering denunciation. Yet his words held terrific conviction.

Suddenly he relapsed. He stared at the floor, trembling violently again, a prey to the terrible malady that had him in its grip.

'You thought it was Eleanor,' he muttered. 'I could have told you. I could have told you. She was as innocent as a babe newly born, poor child. And then when the parlourmaid gave her stupid and bigoted evidence, and proved herself a barefaced liar, you turned suspicion on her. But you were afraid to prosecute. And the real murderer escaped. Would to God you had caught him!'

Alec started forward, and caught at Mr Quinny's arm. 'You mean that?' he asked hoarsely. 'You mean that—Eleanor is innocent?'

Mr Quinny peered up through his spectacles. 'My friend,' he said sadly; 'how can you, of all men, think otherwise.'

A hot flush of shame crossed Alec's face. He clenched and unclenched his hands. 'I don't know,' he said wretchedly. 'God help me, I don't know what to think!'

'For my part, knowing what I do of the case, I can hardly believe this,' put in Inspector Brent. 'Why, the man was going to drink port afterwards from the very decanter—'

'Listen, and I will tell you what I know,' said Mr Quinny. He was staring at the floor again intently, and there was a wait of suspense while he seemed to gather himself for the effort. Then he commenced.

'Derek Capel loved Eleanor Appleby, and mad and consuming as his love was for her, so was his hatred for her husband, Professor Appleby. He saw the growing cruelty of the man. He was himself slighted and insulted, for the professor half-guessed his secret. Derek Capel's hatred went hungry for revenge. I know he began to plot the man's death, to think about it, dream about it . . . oh, I know that it was not all unpremeditated.'

Mr Quinny paused, shaking, to hold out his glass. Alec splashed spirit into it with a hand that shook almost as much. But Mr Quinny did not immediately drink it; he stared vacantly at the glass in his hand while he went on.

'Opportunity came that night. Eleanor in her desperation and fear sent round a hurried note to Derek Capel, who was the only person she could think of in her extremity. For I believe he was the only man who dared impose himself in that house.

'The letter was sent by George, the gardener, He was another who had cause to hate Professor Appleby. He said nothing afterwards about conveying that letter, and I don't believe the police ever thought about seriously interrogating him. Old George, the gardener, saw a great deal that went on in that house, and it sickened his soul. He kept a grimly shut mouth about it all afterwards.

'When Derek Capel received that letter, he had to find some pretext for making a call so late that night. And he had one ready at hand. As I say, murder had been in his heart and thoughts for a long time. He had even bought a book on poisons—'

Mr Quinny lifted his head. 'Ah, that makes you start, inspector! That book was never produced at the trial, though Derek Capel himself admitted that he took it late that night to Professor Appleby, who desired to see it.

'There is a curious reason why it was hidden. It is the only part where coincidence comes into the affair at all. For in that book, a rare and valuable edition, by the way, was the recipe for the making of a secret poison that leaves no trace.

Mr Quinny rose and hobbled slowly over to the wainscotting of the wall near the door. He bent down and fumbled with a shaking hand, while his audience watched in fascinated horror. And presently there was a slight click, and a panel flew open.

From the cavity thus revealed, he took a leather-bound volume, and with it in his hand he made his way painfully back, by the aid of his stick, to his seat.

He took up his glass again.

'This is the book on poisons. It is an important piece of evidence. I will now tell you what happened when Derek Capel arrived at Professor Appleby's house.

'He was greeted by the professor, who was alone. His wife had retired to her room. But, because he loved to taunt and sneer, the professor sent a maid up to call her down again. I suppose he wanted to watch the tortures of the man who loved this woman, and desired her for himself.

'Anyhow it was his undoing. It drove Derek Capel mad to see the stress of fear under which she was suffering that night.

'For a few moments Professor Appleby forgot his malignant subtleties in examining the book Derek Capel had brought. Now mark you, here is the curious part. It turned out that he himself had produced, by experiment, the very same secret poison that is mentioned in this book. He pointed out the poison. It was contained in a little blue-black bottle on the shelves.'

Mr Quinny stopped, under the stress of a great excitement, and while the clock ticked audibly, he fumbled at his waistcoat pocket and produced a small tin box, which he opened. From this he took a pill—presumably of quinine, or some other medicine—and dropped it in his glass.

He did not drink, however, but peered at the glass intently for a moment. Then he looked up, his face livid, his eyes staring behind their spectacles at the balcony. But there was no one there now.

'This is the truth. The professor asked his wife to take down the bottle, but when her hand was on it, he arrested it, making some sneering remark about the dangers of poison in her hands. That was the only time she touched the bottle to my knowledge, and that was how her finger-prints came upon it.

'The professor invited his guest to join him in a drink,' went on the strange Mr Quinny in a lowered voice. 'He turned away to the decanters, and Derek Capel took this chance to lean across and whisper to Eleanor. The professor saw a reflection of that action in a mirror hanging over the wall. He came back, poured out port for himself and whisky for Derek Capel—and in the moment of toasting, charged his wife in the most ugly terms with infidelity and ordered her up to her room.

'He went with her, grasping her arm,' went on this mysteriously omniscient stranger. 'He escorted her half-way up the stairs . . . and in the interval of time thus allowed him, Derek Capel seized his opportunity to kill Professor Appleby. He took the poison bottle in his gloved hands, emptied some of the contents into the glass of port, and the remainder into the decanter.'

'Good Heavens!' burst from Alec Portal.

Mr Quinny raised a shaking hand for silence.

'I think Derek Capel was a little bit mad just then. He did not reason everything out so cunningly. He did not plot to get away with his crime. There was a quarrel between him and the professor, and he left the house. But he waited—until he heard screams and shouts, the crash of a falling body. Then he came back, to be in at the death as it were'—Mr Quinny's lips writhed in a mirthless smile at his own grim joke.

'He wanted to commit suicide then. You see he had a moment of bravery. He thought that the contents of the decanter would be analysed, poison would be found in it, and all the evidence would point towards his guilt. So he took up the decanter to pour out his own death drink.'

Mr Quinny shuddered and stared round him with unseeing eyes. Those same peering eyes fixed at last on the glass in his hand. But then with a start he looked up.

'That brings us to the crucial point. It was then, I suppose, that Eleanor Appleby had a flash of intuition, and half-guessed what Derek Capel had done—and what his intentions were. She snatched the decanter from his hands and dropped it.'

A concerted sound that was half a gasp, half a sigh came from his listeners in the room.

Mr Quinny all at once became very listless. He stared hard at the floor, making no effort to check the convulsive tremors that ran through his body. Once he peered at the glass he held in his hand and half-raised it to his lips, then set it down again in a fit of violent shuddering.

He looked up. 'That is the story, ladies and gentlemen. The rest I think you know. How Eleanor Appleby was tried for the murder of her husband, and of her acquittal. If she held back any secret, it was her own half-knowledge that Derek Capel was the real murderer. She did not know for certain, but she would not betray him by word or by look. Imagine her anguish of mind! She almost believed that he had done it for her sake. That letter she had sent in the stress of her terror and fear—she could not tell whether it had spurred him to this mad deed or not. She did not know. Bravely, nobly, she prepared herself to take the consequences for it, however.

'And Derek Capel! God, how he paid for his crime! He watched and prayed and hoped during the course of the trial. He went through Hell. But always he was the schemer. There was no altruistic motive in the man. He murdered Professor Appleby because he coveted his wife. And he had the brazen effrontery, the supreme egotistical callousness to watch the woman he loved suffering the tortures of the damned, hoping that she would go free and that he would win her in the end.'

At this point Mr Quinny was forced to stop, overcome by a fit of coughing. It was not a nice sound.

'Gentlemen,' he resumed at last in a choking voice, 'I still maintain that Professor Appleby was a vile creature, and his death was a riddance for the good of humanity. But God's punishment swiftly overtook the man who sought to interfere in His providence. Derek Capel was defeated by his own ends. He saw the woman he loved give her heart to another.' He peered over at Alec Portal. 'She loved you, my friend,' he said sadly. 'She came to rely on you during those dreadful weeks and months, and to think of you as her saviour. And Derek Capel watched it—saw himself losing her and drained his cup of bitterness to the dregs.'

As he finished speaking, Mr Quinny raised his glass to his lips, and with his peering eyes fixed on Alec Portal he gulped down its contents in a paroxysm of trembling.

Seized by a sudden awful foreboding, a prescience of the staggering truth, Alec Portal raised himself from his seat and in a bound crossed over to Mr Quinny.

'What have you done?' he cried, staring in horror and dawning understanding at the shaking wreck of humanity before him. 'Who are you? How do you know these things? Heavens, man, speak—speak!'

Mr Quinny was suddenly stricken by a silent, animal-like frenzy. With gasping, choking breath he tore at his collar, his necktie; his face became gray and empurpled; his spectacles dropped revealing eyes that were glazed and rolling in their sockets. No one could doubt but that he was in his death throes.

He closed his eyes at last, his breathing coming in a dry rattle.

'Come closer, my friend,' he whispered hoarsely. 'Come closer. Everything is going black. There is need for haste. I feel that—she—is—in—danger!'

His eyelids flickered upwards as Alec bent over him, and he smiled a little twisted smile.

'Do you know me, my friend?' he whispered. 'I am Derek Capel, I killed Professor Appleby because I loved her—loved her! I am going out now, Alec—I have just taken a dose of that very same poison. But try to think kindly of me. When I heard you were married, and that letter was locked in the drawer, I came back. I found that letter today, I saw you were unhappy . . . and so I came here tonight to try to make amends—'

He seemed to relapse, his eyes closed, his breathing coming

heavily, only to rally again with a start forward, his emaciated hand clutching at Alec's arm.

'Go to her, Alec,' he whispered. 'For Heaven's sake go! She is in danger—I feel it, I know it. She was listening upstairs, and she thinks . . . Oh, God, stop her!' he shrieked suddenly. 'She is there, by the pond!'

He fell back, panting and writhing convulsively, his eyes closed. Alec stared around him, trying desperately to make a clutch at his reeling senses, Eleanor—where was she? Wildly his eyes stared up to the balcony, and then he dashed up the stairs. She was not there, not in her room. The conviction came upon him that Derek Capel was right.

Hatless, and with an awful fear at his heart, he raced out into the grounds.

Fleet as the wind he raced through the shrubberies. He saw her at last, standing at the edge of the lake. She looked like a beautiful wraith in her gown of cream ninon. Her hands were outstretched, and there was a rapt look upon her face. He ran, his heart in his mouth.

'Eleanor!' he called.

She turned, and for a moment she looked like a trapped, desperate creature. But she must have seen something in his face, for she stared and held out her slender white arms to him.

He reached her side and fell at her feet.

'Eleanor, forgive me—forgive me!' he cried. 'I was a blind fool. I should have known you were innocent. But God forgive me, I did not quite believe.'

She touched his head. She uttered his name in a tone singularly low and sweet, and throbbing with gladness.

'Alec—Alec—what shall I say? Oh, how do you know even now?'

He looked up. 'That man, Eleanor. He was Derek Capel. He came to confess—'

For a long moment she was silent, palpitating. When he looked up again the tears were streaming down her face.

He sprang to his feet. 'Eleanor—look at me! Oh, my darling, I can't bear it! Am I past forgiveness? You won't say that. Tell me, Eleanor—'

For answer she came close to him, and hid her face. 'Alec . . . oh, Alec! Take me . . . I shall die if you leave me again.'

'Eleanor!' Her name burst from his lips in a sob of happiness.

He caught her up, and murmuring to her, carried her away into the scented light of the flower-haunted gardens.

THE END

APPENDIX

The Grand Magazine (published by George Newnes)
1. The Passing of Mr Quinn (*aka* The Coming of Mr Quin) – No.229, Mar 1924
2. The Shadow on the Glass – No.236, Oct 1924
3. A Sign in the Sky (*aka* The Sign in the Sky) – No.245, Jun 1925
4. A Man of Magic (*aka* At the 'Bells and Motley') – No.249, Nov 1925

The Story-teller magazine (Cassell & Co.)
5. At the Crossroads (*aka* The Love Detectives) – No.236, Dec 1926
6. The Soul of the Croupier – No.237, Jan 1927
7. The World's End – No.238, Feb 1927
8. The Voice in the Dark – No.239, Mar 1927
9. The Face of Helen – No.240, Apr 1927
10. Harlequin's Lane – No.241, May 1927

The Grand Magazine (George Newnes)
11. The Dead Harlequin – No.288, Mar 1929

Britannia & Eve magazine (British National Newspapers)
12. The Man from the Sea – Vol.1 No.6, Oct 1929

The Mysterious Mr Quin (W. Collins Sons & Co.)
13. The Bird with the Broken Wing – Apr 1930

Winter's Crimes No.3 (Macmillan & Co.)
14. The Harlequin Tea Set – Nov 1971

THE MYSTERIOUS MR QUIN

AGATHA CHRISTIE

MR SATTERTHWAITE is a dried-up elderly little man who has never known romance or adventure himself. He is a looker-on at life. But he feels an increasing desire to play a part in the drama of other people—especially is he drawn to mysteries of unsolved crime. And here he has a helper—the mysterious Mr Quin—the man who appears from nowhere—who 'comes and goes' like the invisible Harlequin of old. Who is Mr Quin? No one knows, but he is one who 'speaks for the dead who cannot speak for themselves', and he is also the friend of lovers. Prompted by his mystic influence. Mr Satterthwaite plays a real part in life at last, and unravels mysteries that seem incapable of solution. In Mr Quin, Agatha Christie has created a character as fascinating as Hercule Poirot himself.